HUMBLE MEETINGS

THE SECOND HUMBLE GREETINGS NOVEL

ESSIE POWERS

AFTER MIDNIGHT

*S*itting up in bed, propped up by several well-plumped pillows, Harriet Tumblebeach turned the page of the book she was reading. The *rustle* of the page was nearly deafening in the silent bedroom. It had been well after midnight when Harriet had woken with a start. She had been covered in a thin layer of sweat. The air was still stifling in her bedroom, even though she had thrown the window wide open before lying down on the mattress a few hours ago. Why was it that these long Normonswold summers just went on and on? She thought about how in the winters everyone was constantly talking about the wonders of summer, and how it would illuminate everyone's mood . . . nobody ever seemed to remember the sensations like this. The countless sleepless nights when the humid atmosphere wouldn't let a person have anything other than the most superficial rest.

Harriet shifted herself out of bed, walking to the window. Her blond hair hung down like a pair of damp drapes. Outside, there was no discernible breeze — not even an arid one. Everything was still. She looked out of the window, across at the stables. She breathed in the thick stench of the horses her aunt — Adiema Smith — kept. When Harriet held her breath, she thought she could hear them respiring gently — dreaming their equine dreams. A little further away, she made out the riding pen. The dry sawdust which lined the ground seemed to carry on the air she breathed, lining her throat and nostrils.

She crossed the room, sticking her head out of the window which looked down onto the darkened village street. As expected, she saw no one and nothing.

That was the thing about Normonswold, it wasn't anything like living in a city. When the village went to bed, it seemed almost as if life itself came grinding to a halt. There were no all-night bars, or cafes . . . there weren't even any streetlamps. Just pitch darkness, mitigated only by the odd porchlight which'd been left on. But this was the life she had chosen, or so it seemed. She had decided to stay behind, for good or ill, and she could blame no one but herself for the consequences.

Blaming someone else would've been no way to live.

Even in her thinnest nightdress, Harriet felt smothered as she shifted her way along the landing, doing her best not to wake her sleeping aunt. She felt Maximilian — their ginger cat — rub himself up against her calves. He let out a slight *burr* of greeting and the two of them descended the staircase to the kitchen.

As always in summer, her aunt had made a pitcher of lemonade and left it in the fridge. Harriet poured herself a glass and then took a seat at one end of the kitchen table. Maximilian continued to brush against her leg, clearly hopeful that Harriet might see her way to filling up his food bowl — an early serving of breakfast . . . Harriet, however, felt strangely weak; a lot weaker than she had felt for a long time. There was something about the summer heat which sapped her strength — which made her light-headed. Sometimes she longed for the coming winter. Perhaps then she would feel better.

It was true to say that the events of the past few months had been giddying. How they had chased Lord Charles Knightly out of Normonswold with nothing but the power of protest . . . and, of course, the help from the anonymous souls who had opened the golf resort's septic tanks.

In a strange way, Harriet felt a longing for a return to those times. She had felt so alive on the picket line, blocking the arrival of construction vehicles, and feeling the warmth of the bond she had formed with the other women. Now, though, it seemed that life had returned to much as it had been previously. Now, there was nothing to do but complain about the impossible-to-stand heat.

Thinking on all this and more, Harriet finished up her lemonade, then set the glass down in the sink. Her aunt was always getting at her about doing 'unnecessary' washing-up, claiming that for a young, single lady such as herself it would only damage her dove-soft skin, and — by extension — her hope of ever finding anyone, and — again by extension — her hope of ever being happy. In greater moments of clarity, Harriet wondered just what her aunt knew about this — having decided decades ago that her only life companions would be a housecat and a stable of horses.

Having finished her lemonade, Harriet felt strangely directionless. She couldn't face going back to bed. She had already been reading for hours. And it was too early for her to take a shower and prepare for the day ahead — the racket would without a doubt wake her aunt — she decided to throw caution to the wind, plucking her overcoat off the hook by the door, popping a pair of battered trainers onto her feet, and venturing out into the village.

Light was just beginning to creep over the horizon. And there was that familiar sense of a new dawn approaching. There was still not so much as a breeze, but it felt better to be out in the open, somehow, even if it was only to find herself beneath an oppressive layer of cloud. Harriet walked to the edge of the village, finding the quiet pond where she and Bella had so often come together to lie in the sun and to speak about whatever was on their minds: usually boys, parents and school, in that order.

Harriet thought of lying on the grassy bank, but she was worried someone out early walking their dog might see. She had to think of those things in a village as small as Normonswold. No matter how comfortable she ever deigned to feel, it was unmistakeable that there was always someone — *somewhere* — watching on and judging her . . . not that Harriet would know until gossip began to float about town.

No, Harriet had to control herself.

She had to be an *adult* . . . whatever that really meant.

It was only as the daylight became bright enough to see the horizon that Harriet decided she should be heading back home.

When she got back home, she glanced at the clock and realised that it was an acceptable time for her to turn on the shower without risk of waking her aunt. Even when she ran cold water over her body, Harriet felt as if her blood was on fire. Even once she had dabbed herself dry and set her mind to working on what she would wear that day, she felt strangely empty . . . perhaps it was the lack of sleep, that was usually the culprit . . . well, there was nothing to do about that now.

She had to go to work.

And there would be no naptime there.

In the end, she decided on a sensible pair of trousers with a floaty cream blouse to wear over the top, then she went downstairs to whip herself together some breakfast from nothing but a banana, a handful of granola and a splash of milk.

All the while, Maximilian watched on in great expectation, until Harriet caught the clue and served him his breakfast. He purred noisily and pressed himself hard up against her shins. Despite having woken early, Harriet barely had time to brush her teeth and go through the final preparations for leaving the house before she heard the pair of pips on the car horn outside. Glancing up the stairs, and willing her aunt not to wake, she wormed her way out of the front door and to the waiting car.

2

THE WORKING DAY

*A*s always, Dorothy or — as he was known on weekdays — Kieran was dressed in a finely pressed suit. His tie knotted to his throat. Still, despite the image of normality which Dorothy projected day-to-day, there was still the matter of his car.

It was just like any other hatchback, except for the fact that the air stank of peaches and cream; a teddy-bear shaped car freshener hung from the rear-view mirror; and the car seats and steering wheel were covered in a fuzzy, deep-purple material. She had heard people — many times over — discussing Dorothy's car, and how it must belong to his non-existent daughter because there was no other explanation for the décor. One thing was for certain, as far as the people at work were concerned, the only person who existed was Kieran Eric Doores. The only person in the office who knew the truth was Harriet.

It was a good thirty-five minutes to their office in Yillingford. Dorothy had taken advantage of the there-and-back-again daily commutes to get to know Harriet's love life on an intimate level —

not that there was all that much to know. In return, however, Harriet felt that she had learned absolutely nothing about Dorothy. Only that he had a penchant for cross-dressing which she had always assumed shrouded some childhood trauma or other.

Harriet didn't like to pry.

But that didn't mean that Dorothy would return the favour.

"Any new prospects?" Dorothy asked, flipping the indicator so that they took the exit to the offices of Autumn International: Paving Slabs and Outdoor Ornaments.

Even despite all this time — even after Harriet had opened up about so much of her past to Dorothy — she couldn't help but feel herself begin to blush.

"In Normonswold, you mean?" she asked. "I've seen a few ducks down at the pond who look as if they're after a life mate."

Dorothy rolled his eyes. He guided the car through a roundabout, joining the queue for the office car park. Already Harriet recognised the odd grey face beneath glass — her co-workers making their way into the office this Monday morning. She did her best not to catch anyone's eye, wanting to suspend the feeling of freedom the weekend inspired in her for just a few minutes longer. "You've got to make opportunities," Dorothy went on. "It's no good for you to mooch about your aunt's house looking all mopey in nothing but the company of a cat."

"You sound like you've been spying on me."

Dorothy grinned, pulling into a space alongside a convertible which Harriet knew belonged to their boss, Clive. "I've always been very observant — there's nothing shameful about that. I just want everyone to be their best self."

"And that involves me shacking up with someone else, does it?"

"Well," Dorothy said, turning off the engine and pulling the keys from the ignition, "do you honestly feel fulfilled in nothing but your aunt's company right now?"

It was true, there was nothing Harriet could say to that; and so, feeling plucky that particular morning — maybe because she'd got up so early — she decided to fight back. "If being with someone else is so great, then how come you never settled down?"

Dorothy sat still at the wheel for a long few moments, staring ahead through the windscreen to their fellow colleagues passing by outside. "Some of us just don't have any luck." His sombre tone lasted for only a matter of seconds as he turned to face her, a slight smile parting his lips. "Don't tell me you're not even going to *try*."

As always, the offices at Autumn International: Paving Slabs and Outdoor Ornaments were bustling with activity. To be quite honest, although she often complained about her job to anybody who cared to listen, she secretly savoured the opportunity it offered her . . . to forget everything and plunge herself into monotonous, brainless routine.

Without any conscious effort, she swiped up armfuls of paper and flushed them into neat piles, slotting them into trays she didn't even need to look at. By the time she had made it back to her desk, it was close to ten o'clock. That was the wonderful thing about her job; it was so busy that time just seemed to *fly* by . . .

While she sifted through her email, she joined in on the conversation her colleagues were having about the heat. Although she mentioned that it was keeping her up at night — not allowing her a decent sleep — she said nothing about having got dressed and walked into the village; that was a Little Weird, and she knew that anything that was a Little Weird would be picked up on and noted by someone somewhere, and would come back to haunt her at a later date. Oh it might not be anything conscious, nobody would *point* to something which she had exactly said — word for word — but the feeling in the air would be that Harriet was a bit kooky, or slightly left-of-centre. Such things were not valued commodities in the Autumn International: Paving Slabs and Outdoor Ornaments offices.

It was a wonder that Dorothy managed to present such a straight-laced image of himself to the world . . . that Kieran Eric Doores managed to pack Dorothy away so successfully during the working day.

If only Harriet could be as savvy as Dorothy.

It was nearing lunch when Harriet felt someone looking at her. It wasn't quite a sixth sense. And certainly nothing a Little Weird. She had heard that lots of people possessed the ability of knowing when they were the centre of attention. She glanced over her shoulder, realising that her boss, Clive, was determinedly making his way over to her desk.

Knowing how often she wrongly attributed her boss's attention to herself, and not to another of her colleagues, Harriet returned to work. She returned to the email she was writing to one of their customers, about how Autumn International: Paving Slabs and Outdoor Ornaments 'deeply regretted' their 'customer experience' and how they were looking to 'put it right by any reasonable means possible'.

"Harriet?"

Her blood froze. It was that same sensation Harriet would experience back at school, when a teacher would call her name. She was loath to turn her head, wanting to delay the interaction for as long as possible. In the end, though, it was inevitable that she

9

had to participate in the exchange. She turned her chair around to see her boss.

As always, Clive's appearance was flawless. His suit was well-tailored, his fingernails manicured and what remained of his hair slicked back with gel. His black eyes had a way of seeing you without *really* seeing you. It was always as if he was looking just over your shoulder at something slightly more interesting.

"Would you see me in my office before the end of the day?"

Harriet blinked once — twice — and then she nodded.

When Clive had returned to his office, across the floor, Harriet went back to her email. She continued as if nothing at all had even happened.

Later that day, Harriet was trembling when she rapped her knuckles against the door to Clive's office. As was always the case, he had left his door open during the morning before shutting it for most of the afternoon. This was because he spent a large portion of the afternoon on the phone to Important Clients . . . clients who merited a more personalised service than that which his under-lings could provide.

As Clive called Harriet inside, she instinctively glanced to Dorothy, seeing him sitting at a desk nearby, where he worked as a supervisor. He gave her a long, sympathetic stare, and for the first time Harriet felt grave misgivings about the meeting which was to take place.

"Sit down, Harriet, please."

Harriet settled in the chair arranged in front of Clive's desk. The window behind Clive's chair looked out over the car park. A little way in the distance, though, she realised she could make out trees . . . the beginnings of a forest. Already, not watching herself too carefully, Harriet felt her mind itching to escape. To submerge itself completely in the realms of fantasy.

"You will no doubt have noticed how things are at present for Autumn International, Harriet. What the current financial climate means for the company."

Harriet said nothing in reply. To be quite honest, ever since she had started working here — ten years ago now — there had always been a 'financial climate' of something or other. And it was almost never a good thing for Autumn International. She had come to believe that Autumn International was simply not designed for the modern business world. That it was too inflexible, too clumsy, to adapt to change.

This wasn't the answer Clive wanted to hear, however, so Harriet looked Clive in the eye and said, "I have noticed."

Clive nodded to himself. A slight smile formed on his lips. "If there's one thing I've learned from all my time working here, it's that the world never stands still. It's how we react which will define scope and success in the future."

Not really sure what Clive wanted to hear, Harriet just nodded in response.

Clive's smile faltered and then vanished completely. He reached for a pencil which was lying on his desk and began to roll it back and forth beneath his palm. "You have been here for well over ten years now, Harriet, and I thought that it was well past time that we have a chat about how . . . how things are going."

Harriet said nothing, watching the pencil which Clive kept pinned beneath his palm.

Clive continued, "Do you feel that your career is *progressing*?"

Realising that something was expected of her, she looked back at Clive — again feeling that he was evading her direct stare. "I . . . it depends on what you mean by progressing, I suppose."

Harriet grimaced, knowing this was just one of those things which a person — an *employee* — was just never supposed to say. At the workplace, you accepted questions for what they were. You never pried into messy matters like pinning down definitions . . .

Clive, however, seemed faintly tickled by this. He smiled again. This time the smile didn't instantly leave his face. "Well, we could take it by the traditionally understood meaning, which is, I imagine, to *move forward* . . . would you say that your career is *moving forward*, Harriet?"

Harriet held herself still, very aware of her breathing — of how she drew air deeply into her lungs, and how it expanded her chest outwards. She shuddered slightly when she exhaled. To tell the truth, she had been doing more or less the same job ever since she had come here. She never really thought about it. She just showed up, did what she was told, and what she knew herself to be responsible for, and then she left. "No," she said, in a quiet voice. "I wouldn't say my career's moving forward."

Clive reclined slightly in his chair, relinquishing his hold on the pencil. "And does that not concern you?"

Harriet wanted to reply that it didn't concern her in the slightest, but again she knew that brutal honesty was something that just wouldn't fly at Autumn International, or any workplace for that matter. "I've . . . never been all that . . . ambitious . . ."

The words hung in Clive's office for the longest time, and Harriet already felt that she had made a misstep. No taking them back now.

Clive held himself poised, then reached into one of his desk drawers and slipped out an envelope stamped 'PRIVATE AND CONFIDENTIAL'. "There's a saying which I've always disagreed with. It's the one which goes, 'Fake it until you make it.' I believe that this one saying is answerable to huge damage throughout our society by those who think that by showing up, by putting on a brave face, and getting the job done, will get them somewhere. But it won't. If there is no deep-rooted *passion* for what one does then there will never be true success. Do you not agree, Harriet?"

Harriet said nothing.

Clive pursed his lips and slid the envelope across the desk. "What we're offering, Harriet, is a very attractive redundancy package — I would be most pleased if you would look it over and tell me what you think."

Harriet looked down at the pages which Clive was passing to her. Despite the seeming important of this moment — in her career, in her *life* — she just couldn't bring herself to look any further than the Autumn International logo on the front of the envelope. It might not even have been addressed to her for all she knew.

Finally, she managed to raise her voice. "Do I need to come into work tomorrow?"

"You will find all of the terms laid out in the letter, Harriet."

She paused a second longer before taking the envelope and leaving the office.

3

BREAKING POINT

Since there wasn't anything else for Harriet to do in the next few days, she found herself venturing each morning to Old Couple's Café, down Disjointed Lane, off Normonswold High Street. Just so that she would get out of the house. Each day, she ordered a latte and then took to sipping at it while she browsed the previous day's newspaper for job advertisements. It was difficult for her to properly take in the text before her, it was as if the inky blobs all kept growing legs and wandering about on the page.

The words just wouldn't stay *still*.

Every day it was always the same, after about fifteen minutes of solid, unrewarded effort, she would give up and sweep the newspaper to one side, deciding to dedicate herself to absorbing the décor of Old Couple's Café.

Ever since Harriet could remember the place, she had thought it somewhat corny. The titular Old Couple was Geoffrey and Diana

Banks. Pictures of themselves were hung on the walls, documenting the various journeys they had taken throughout their life together — trips to the Berlin Wall, the Coliseum in Rome, and the Empire State Building. There was something which tickled her about the name of the café, given that Geoffrey and Diana couldn't have been much over fifty when they opened it; they now had to both be well into their eighties. Was it really true that you spent thirty years of your life being 'old'? If so, then when did the 'being young' period end?

How much longer did she have?

Feeling as if she was being sucked into an invisible pool of quicksand, Harriet remembered back when Bella had worked here while they'd both been at school. She recalled how Bella had asked permission to give Harriet a free coffee every couple of hours, when she came here bearing her school textbooks.

It all seemed a lifetime ago.

It was as if the time for joking — and for laughter — had passed.

Now she needed to grow up.

Shouldn't what had happened today be the most startling wake-up call of her life?

She had slept through the first ten years of her career while — unbeknownst to her — someone had been taking notes all the while . . . observing her closely. And now she had lost what had — for better or worse — provided the foundation of her life; her financial stability. Autumn International: Paving Slabs and Outdoor Ornaments wasn't much, but it had kept her ticking over for what felt like the longest time.

And now she was leaving all of that security behind.

Because Harriet couldn't focus any longer, and she was afraid that she might explode if she didn't speak to *someone*, she slipped her phone out of her handbag. She flipped through the screens, picked out Dorothy's number, and dialled.

When Dorothy had asked her if things were as bad as he had expected on the car journey home, Harriet had merely shown him the envelope which Clive had handed her . . . the one which contained the terms of her redundancy. He had told her to take her time. To have some rest. To get in touch if she wanted to talk.

When she heard Dorothy's voice on the other end of the line, Harriet felt herself already beginning to relax. Before Harriet could say anything of any substance, Dorothy declared that he was coming by to pick her up right away. True to his word, within fifteen minutes, he pulled up outside, and then stepped into the café.

Instead of plonking himself down on the chair opposite, he reached for her arm, helping her out of her seat. Here it seemed as if 'helping' was something of a euphemism since Dorothy in reality had a good go at yanking her arm clean out of its socket. Leaving Dorothy's car behind parked on the pavement, the two of them marched arm-in-arm to what — as it turned out — was a preordained destination: Molinaar's Cottage; what had once been the home of Florianette Rutherford and her boutique shop Modern Styles, but which was now where Bella's venture, Humble Greetings, had sunk its roots.

Harriet hung back as they stood on the doorstep. She was unsure. She didn't know if she was ready to let anyone else know about what had happened to her. She had only told her aunt so far. And she could trust her aunt to keep the news to herself. Her logical mind told her that everybody was going to know sooner or later . . . so why not *sooner* rather than later?

Dorothy gave her the encouragement that she might've been lacking, leading the two of them — step-by-step — up to the front door and then throwing the knocker three times, brutally efficient and powerful. There was something about Dorothy which always frustrated Harriet. She supposed it was the way that he seemed to have everything worked out; he was utterly at peace with himself and his place in the world. As if he no longer cared for anything but his own happiness. Harriet felt a rather large pang of jealousy.

It was Bella who came to the door. And there was something so pleasant — so *happy* — about the expression on her face that it was all Harriet could do to keep herself from breaking down into sobs right there and then.

And then her strength deserted her.

It took two glasses of something sweet and citric before Harriet returned to something resembling consciousness. She wasn't entirely sure what had happened.

She was sitting in the garden of Molinaar's Cottage, in the shade of a large oak tree, while Bella, Dorothy and now Cassandra — the teenage designer Bella had hired — all stood around her looking extremely concerned. She hadn't fainted; she had stayed on her feet. But there had been something — some *essence* — which had deserted her. She had gone all weak. It had only been Dorothy's firm hold which had prevented her from dropping to the ground.

"Give her room, give her room," Dorothy said, using his arms to create a makeshift barrier . . . as if Dorothy himself wasn't guilty of being just a *little* too close. "Drink," Dorothy said.

Harriet once more became conscious of the cool glass in her hand. She brought it up to her lips and sipped. It sent a shudder through her — but a welcome one. She gradually felt life returning to her limbs; the blood beginning to pump back around her body. She took deep breaths, trying to get her brain back into the present moment.

Trying to bring her mind back to *Earth*.

"Okay, okay . . . okay," Harriet mumbled to herself. And then, because nothing else occurred to her, she looked to Bella and asked, "Where's Robert?"

Bella blinked a few times, as if clearing a daze. "Oh, he's out for the day. He'll be back before evening."

Harriet thought about how often she had quietly admired their relationship, and the responsibility the two of them shared with their joint venture of Humble Greetings. She wondered why she had never been able to be as sure in herself and in her desires as Bella and Robert always seemed to be. Harriet was nothing but a *disaster* by comparison.

But that didn't mean she was going to break down.

No.

She would stay strong.

And it was with that thought firmly etched upon her mind that — against a background of protests for her to stay where she was — she rose up out of the chair, still gripping the cool glass she had been given. She felt surer now. *Steadier* on her feet. She looked about the garden, noting how the flowers had come into bloom, and how the grass was thick and lush. She looked down at her feet, realising that she was still wearing slip-on shoes. She took them off and then spread her toes among the grass. She was all too aware of the others watching from over her shoulder. But she didn't care. She was happy for them to draw whatever conclusions they saw fit. The way she saw it, she had already made such a fool of herself that just a little more idiocy would hardly make a scrap of difference.

Harriet strolled around the garden, feeling the beginnings of a light breeze blowing over the roofs of the surrounding houses. It was pleasant, and it was relaxing. She knew that she must appear like some insane performing artist, making a spectacle of herself like this; just treading her way about the garden, a vague smile on her face . . . it was a wonder nobody saw fit to call an ambulance.

When Harriet had completed a circuit, however, she felt much better than she had in years. Perhaps the news she had received was finally beginning to sink in — perhaps the *truth* of it was beginning to sink in. For better or for worse, she was going to be free.

Free.

Didn't that mean that she had 'won' in some strange way?

That she was going out on her own terms?

It was only when she returned to the chair where she had been sitting that the weariness within her began to take hold. 'Weariness' was one way to put it . . . she felt as if she had just run back-to-back marathons.

Before Harriet got a chance to sit — and perhaps worried that if Harriet did take a seat that she would never get back up again — Bella took gentle hold of the crook of her arm, and said, "Would you like to see our latest designs?"

4

A NEW START

*I*t was incredible to think that the studio had once featured all of Florianette Rutherford's latest conjurings; the designs which she had held within her her entire life, and which she had finally decided to let loose on the unsuspecting village of Normonswold with her shop: Modern Styles. Following her death, Bella had repurposed Molinaar's Cottage as a design studio for greetings cards. The studio in its current guise featured a pair of desks: one for Cassandra — the illustrator — and another for Bella — the writer. There were several framed cards Humble had produced on the walls.

One which particularly caught Harriet's fancy featured a bear holding its honey-dripping fingers above its head and sucking at the ooze as it dangled down. There were two cards pasted beside one another within the frame; one which showed off the illustration on the front cover, and another which displayed the message inside.

Harriet read what was written:

Help runs from our hands,
From mine to yours,
Birthday wishes; forever more.

Harriet had been drawn in by the card because she had received it from Casandra and Bella for her birthday. She recalled how when she had received the card she had spent a long minute or so just staring at the message, trying to work out what it meant. There was definitely something obscure, and yet she supposed Bella had always operated in this way.

She had always had a cryptic side to her.

Also, Harriet had been particularly pleased with the card because everyone seemed to gather from seemingly nothing more than the fact that she lived with her aunt at her riding stables that she was a horse lover, and that she would like nothing more than a birthday card generously endowed with horses. In many ways, Harriet felt guilty about her situation. She knew that there must be countless girls and young women who would've been positively giddy at the prospect of living in such close proximity with horses.

But what could Harriet do? She really had no other place to go . . . and now that she had no job, there was little prospect of her being able to do what she had always *said* she would do, which was to move away . . .

"Like that one?" Bella asked.

"Hmm? Uh, yeah, of course. I recognise it. From my birthday."

Bella smiled wide. "I'm glad you didn't forget — I guess greetings cards have a little more staying power than they're given credit for."

Harriet looked around for Dorothy, with the vague notion that she might quite like to get going home now. Although she knew it was somewhat pathetic, she was looking forward to just getting back and snuggling up on the sofa with a hot water bottle, blanket and Maximilian purring away on her lap.

"We were wondering if you'd like a job," Bella said, from out of nowhere.

Harriet turned back to Bella. "What did you say?"

"A job? Would you like to work for Humble?"

Harriet thought it over a few moments. She was already on the brink of shaking her head. "I'm not a very good employee — not based on what happened to me last week."

"You were utilised wrongly. I think we'd find better ways of allocating your talents."

Although Harriet's first response was to answer back, *What talents?*, she maintained her silence. She glanced about the studio space, already imagining a desk of her own among them. Why did it give her a strange, warming sensation in the pit of her stomach to think of herself working with Bella — her best friend from school? She supposed that one part of it was nostalgia. But there was still the nagging voice at the back of her head which told her that this was somehow a big mistake or, worse, a joke at her expense.

"Look," Bella went on, "what's the worst that can happen? If you're as rubbish as you say then I'll sack you. Okay?"

Even though Harriet was sure that this was nothing but a terrible idea, she found herself agreeing. "Okay."

"Good," Bella said, looking to Dorothy and Cassandra who — clearly in on the idea from the very start — were grinning all over too. "Now that's settled, I think we should celebrate, don't you think?"

Robert turned up later on, and the celebrations commenced.

The celebrations featured a bottle of champagne which had somehow snuck its way into the kitchen from what was supposed to have been the Grand Opening of the Knightly Resort and Leisure Complex. It hadn't turned out to be much of a 'grand opening' at all when someone had let loose the contents of a pair of septic tanks.

Harriet had been afraid of drinking alcohol. She had had the notion that it would send her either one way or another; into manic depression, or else into a fit of hysterics and impossible-to-control high spirits.

Both would have led to the same gnawing hole of paranoid fear by the next day.

As it turned out, the champagne sent her along neither path. All it did was pleasantly warm her whole body and fill her with a general sense of well-being. When someone knocked at the door at what must've been after ten at night, Harriet had a fresh bounce in her step as she volunteered to go answer.

She wasn't certain who she had been expecting to find on the doorstep — perhaps she had half convinced herself that her Aunt Adiema had gone out walking in the village, searching for her missing niece.

However, it wasn't her aunt.

She recognised him instantly, of course. The only block in her mind was the one which told her — instinctively — that there was no reason for him to be here.

Not now.

It was George, personal assistant to Lord Charles Knightly.

There was something . . . different about George.

Had he always had such chiselled cheekbones? Such a defined

neckline? Had his shirts previously clung so tightly to such well-worked pectoral muscles?

She noticed also that, whereas previously he had had something of an afro growing from his scalp, he had now buzzed his hair close to the skin. Although she had never thought of herself as the type to go for bald men, there was certainly something about seeing George like this. An element of danger mixed in with the soft personality she knew him to possess . . .

"Erm, hello?" George said, that familiar bounce to his voice. "Is Bella here at all?"

Harriet returned to reality. She had to remind herself that this was the enemy. And that she was in danger of fraternisation. "Why'd you want to know?"

"I . . . wanted to have a chat with her."

Feeling buffed up by the champagne she'd drunk, Harriet shook her head. "I'm sorry — you're going to have to do better than that."

"I have a proposal for her."

"She's finished with Lord Charles."

"I'm . . . not working for Lord Charles anymore."

Harriet opened and then shut her mouth. She wasn't sure what to say. She had been so clear in her mind what she was going to say next. And then she was going to take great joy in throwing the front door shut in his face.

Now, though, everything was changed.

"Why're you here, then?"

George — clearly growing a touch exasperated — said, "To speak with Bella." He attempted to look past her, and Harriet couldn't help but get a brief glimpse of his washboard stomach as his shirt rode up his body. "She *asked* me to come."

"You're looking different," Harriet said, before she could stop herself.

Giving up his attempts to get in touch with Bella, however briefly, George switched his attention back onto her. His expression softened slightly. "I've been in Australia for a year or so — I wanted to get away from things for a while. Reassess."

"And that reassessment brought you back to Normonswold?"

George's expression was neutral for several moments. Then he said, "Yes."

Harriet felt her heart striking hard against her ribcage. Then she remembered herself. This wasn't her house that George had come to visit, after all. This was Bella's house. And she — and only she — had the last say on who entered or who was turned away.

Before Harriet got into her mind that she needed to turn back to the kitchen, to go and fetch Bella, she heard her familiar voice behind her. "George! Do come in! We're just having some champagne — at the expense of your former employer!"

The moment between them broken — like a rock dropped through the perfectly still surface of a lake — George turned away.

And then Harriet followed.

5

STARTING OUT

*H*arriet had somehow got it into her head that she was going to be doing mundane tasks about the Humble offices — filing, photocopying and sorting — so she was surprised when on her first day Bella asked how she would like to go out and meet a prospective client. It was here Harriet felt it necessary to mention that she didn't drive . . . not since she had failed her test for the seventh time.

This issue wasn't swept away as easily as others had been. Bella took a moment to consider, and then said, "We'll sort that out," before switching tack and suggesting that Robert drive Harriet out to her first assignment.

Although Harriet felt a burden to Humble already, she knew that she could only do what she was told to the best of her ability. And since Humble was based in a small village with just about no public transport connections to anywhere at all, she was somewhat at the mercy of people who could drive.

Before Harriet set out on the road with Robert, Bella took

Harriet by the arm and led her upstairs, to what turned out to be a wardrobe stuffed with trouser suits, and dresses, and blouses, and an array of other formal attire. Bella stood back and waited while Harriet picked out something appropriate. It was a good thing that Harriet and Bella wore pretty much the same size.

Dressed for business, Harriet headed out of the house with Robert, feeling at least a little more normal considering that Robert himself was wearing a suit.

They looked like a power couple.

On the drive, Robert made polite conversation, asking about Harriet's former job, and what she had done before being unceremoniously tossed. It was only as they closed on their destination that Harriet realised the chat was something along the lines of a job interview. By the time they reached the customer's offices, she felt as if she had undergone a thorough — *if gentle* — grilling.

She felt so unnatural doing her best to stride confidently alongside Robert, the two of them falling into a mutual pace. When they greeted the customer, Harriet felt nothing short of a fraud. What did she know about Humble? What business did she have being here and speaking to one of their customers? She was glad Robert did the talking.

As Harriet sat and listened, she did her best to understand everything they talked about, the lines of greetings cards on offer. It turned out that the customer was an owner of several large, independent department stores, and that she was interested in buying a Christmas batch. It surprised Harriet to see how slickly Robert could assume the role of a salesperson, not stopping once he had sold the Christmas cards, pushing his luck by offering a deal for a year-round supply of seasonal greetings cards. The customer agreed to his offer on the spot. Harriet felt like she had been caught up in the trail of a hurricane.

By the time they left the offices behind, Robert made a point of thanking the customer for their time, and introducing Harriet all over again, as if she had been forgotten sitting beside them. When they were back in the car, Robert checked his phone, then glanced up at Harriet with a twinkle in his eye.

"Are you ready for your first lesson?"

"My first what?"

"Your first driving lesson."

Harriet was ready to reply, telling him that she'd already *had* several driving lessons, albeit a long time ago. And that she had failed the test *seven* times. But there was something about Robert's tone of voice, something about his subtle, cocky smile, which told her that it was probably in her best interest not to respond.

They returned to Normonswold, and to the headquarters of Humble at Molinaar's Cottage. Harriet realised she was shaking when she stepped out of Robert's car, and back up the familiar walkway to the front door.

Since Bella and Cassandra were hard at work in the studio, Harriet quietly made her way up the stairs to where she had taken the professional clothes she was wearing. Swiftly and neatly, she replaced the clothes in the wardrobe, then headed back downstairs. She was somewhat surprised to find everyone who worked for Humble standing in the kitchen:

Bella.

Robert.

Cassandra.

. . . George.

Robert was still dressed in his suit. Although he hadn't so much as loosened the knot in his tie, he was leaning down to gently scratch his dog Woss's ears. "George here has some experience of teaching people to drive, don't you George?"

George blushed slightly. He looked Harriet in the eye for the briefest moment, and then glanced back at Robert. This was the first time that Harriet had seen George to be anything but the stuck-up, constantly-in-a-hurry assistant to Lord Charles . . . but, then again, perhaps those were character traits which would've been demanded of any assistant.

"I've done it over a few summers . . . a job on the side."

Harriet couldn't help but feel somewhat embarrassed by this. George was younger than she was, and he had not only learned how to drive, but had been teaching other people *professionally* to do the same. She had always parroted the idea that anybody could do anything they set out to do, if only they applied their mind to the task . . . but now she had to prove it to herself.

Harriet pushed her foot down on the clutch pedal. She could hear the motor rumbling through her whole body. She glanced to George, sat in the passenger seat of his car, and felt a thrill pass through her chest. "Uh, what now?" she asked.

"Put the car into gear," George replied, as if it was the most obvious thing in the world.

And — for all Harriet knew — it was.

She felt like an idiot to have forgotten most of what she had learned, even if the last time she had driven a car had been ten years ago.

She did as George told her and — almost immediately — felt the engine quiver, lurch forward, splutter then stall. She sat gripping the steering wheel, feeling the car completely still around her, the engine ticking over, as if clucking at her mockingly.

She looked to George.

"Try again," he said.

Harriet felt herself shaking now. She thought of all those times when she had stalled cars previously. She thought of how her instructors would be patient to begin with before growing more and more impatient as she failed to show any sign of improvement.

She turned the ignition.

Pressed her foot down, and . . . stalled again.

This time Harriet pushed herself back into the driver's seat, closed her eyes and drew a deep breath. She had to be patient with herself, she knew that . . . and yet it was *so* hard.

All too aware of George observing her, she turned the ignition again, this time managing not to stall. Satisfied with herself, she looked to George who told her what to do next. She followed his instructions, pulling away from the side of the road at a snail's pace.

They drove around the small roads which surrounded Normonswold for an hour or so, and Harriet began to feel something of the familiarity of driving returning. It was during this time that she recalled she had never had much trouble with driving around normally. It was dealing with everyday urban situations where she would come unstuck: parallel parking, stopping and starting in traffic, those sorts of things. She wondered if the fact that she had spent most of her time practising driving in and around Normonswold had counted against her in the many, many driving exams she had taken.

After a little while, George directed her back through the village of Normonswold, and to where he had been parked previously. As Harriet slowed, she expected him to tell her to pull up at the side of the road, to yank on the handbrake and to switch off the ignition. But, instead, he told her to stop in the middle of the road alongside Robert's parked car.

She glanced at George, worried that he had suddenly gone mad — perhaps driven that way by her horrendous driving. When she had assumed the position he had indicated, however, she realised what he was trying to get her to do.

"Time for a little parallel parking," George said, his light tone belying the enormity of the task.

Harriet's whole body shook. She felt as if her heart was tapping away at double time. Her muscles went rigid. She squeezed the steering wheel tighter, as if better contact with the car itself would provide her more success. She channelled out everything but the road ahead and behind, and the sound of George's guiding voice.

"Check your mirrors. Full turn to the right. Gentle on the clutch. Ease up on the gas. Guide your way in . . . bringing the wheel back now . . . bring it straight . . . that's it . . . good . . . good . . . *perfect.*"

It was only when Harriet brought the wheel back into the straightened position that she realised she had done what George had asked of her. Although she had merely followed his instructions, she felt an intense gratitude flood her.

Acting on impulse, she lurched across the handbrake, and pulled George into her, giving him a forceful hug. She felt how George resisted her to begin with, before becoming limper. When Harriet realised herself — realised just what she was *doing* — she released him, straightened up, flushing slightly, and said, "Sorry."

George, flushing too, replied, "No, no, it's okay. Fine. Parking is an emotional business. Quite understandable."

"That's the first time I have ever successfully parallel parked."

The two of them smiled at one another. And then Harriet realised she could see Bella and Robert leaving Molinaar's Cottage.

She supposed they were eager to see whether or not Harriet had brought them back alive — Harriet knew that her driving record was something of an open secret around Normonswold; just as anything taking place in a small town was. She almost tripped over her seatbelt getting out of the car.

When she finally found her feet, she realised she was grinning from ear to ear.

6

REBIRTH

*G*eorge Meltz threw his coat down over the immaculately made bed in the room he was paying for at the Thicket Arms Inn. It felt as if he was glowing — from the inside outwards — and that if he were only to stop concentrating for the minutest of moments he might sail up into the air, leaving the ground behind forever.

He opened the taps in the ensuite bathtub. Almost instantly, he felt the warm waft of air from the hot water. He was still flushing slightly.

It seemed such a luxury to have a space to call his own after the year he had spent in Australia. He had taken part in all of the traditional backpacker fare, staying in youth hostels, spending a season picking fruits off the vine, and it still seemed like a shameful luxury to have his own personal space. Not a bunkroom which he had to share with up to twenty other people. There was one point during his trip Down Under when he had considered staying there for good . . . in the end, though, his naturally conservative nature had surfaced and he had taken the sensible option.

Although he had dearly loved chewing on cherries, mangoes, and pitaya, he could hardly go on picking fruit for the rest of his life; that would've been a horrendous waste of his education and the skills he had acquired in his career thus far. He had reasoned that, with a fresh mind — was it a stretch to say a fresh *spirit*? — he would be able to launch himself anew in the United Kingdom, his home country.

And — as if to throw cold water over any concerns he might've had about returning to the UK after a year-long absence — he had found himself fielding almost non-stop phone calls in the first month of his return. He was granted countless invitations to dinner, informal interviews, and even a ticket to an exclusive exhibition, which clearly held an ulterior motive. And while George would've been delighted to have received even *one* offer of this sort when — leaving education behind — he had set his first foot in the business world, none of the offers resounded as anything more than hollow. In short, it felt as if having been in Lord Charles's employ had somewhat spoiled him. It would be difficult to measure up to an experience such as that one. And that had been when Bella had called.

George poured in a few drops of bubble bath, which soon frothed up in the steady, warm flow of water. He watched for a while as — seemingly out of nowhere — the bubbles multiplied and grew.

He thought about how strange it had been to have been back in his London flat, and to see his phone buzzing its way across the table. When he had picked it up, he had half-expected to see the familiar name of some city bigwig, but when the number showed up as unrecognised, it was hardly remarkable. It was near enough standard practice for Big City people to keep their personal credentials private. He had answered the call with some hesitation — he was running out of ways to say no.

But it had been Bella.

And — somehow — she had sold him.

Although George had had reservations about returning to Normonswold, it seemed that he had put them far from his mind now. He recalled how, during the phone call, Bella had told him he had something to offer Humble — actually, as he recalled, the way she had put it was that Robert saw George as 'pivotal' in Humble's functioning moving forward.

When George had got off the phone, he had been just as stunned that he had accepted as that Bella had called him at all. It had just seemed the right thing to do . . . like skipping off to Australia . . .

The water reached the rim of the bathtub and George turned off the taps. He drew in a deep breath, savouring the warm, billowing steam. His whole body relaxed. He recalled how after a day of constant travel with Lord Charles, his body and mind would feel bruised and beaten. As if his job was slowly but surely killing him. Now, though, he felt exactly the opposite. As if he was being . . . *regenerated.*

George undressed, leaving his clothes in a pile to be taken down to reception for laundering. That was something else he had missed greatly during his year in Australia — the access to laundry facilities. Although he had no aversion to hard work, and all of the blood, sweat and tears that entailed, there was something divine about getting clean after all the energy had been expended.

As George stepped into the bath, and allowed himself to gradually sink beneath the bubbles, he realised the warmth he felt in the pit of his stomach had nothing at all to do with the hot water. He wondered if — this time — he hadn't found someone truly special.

7

ON-THE-JOB TRAINING

*H*arriet had got so used to her old job — to the daily grind of prising herself out from between the sheets, into the shower, and then out the door — that she had assumed her job with Humble would soon turn out to be the same deal . . . albeit with her boss being a lifelong friend. However, it was surprising to feel a growing sense of drive with each passing day. She felt as if she positively *bounced* out of bed . . . each morning a little higher, each morning with a greater spring in her step.

One morning, as Harriet gradually brought herself around at the kitchen table, with Maximilian lying in her lap, purring his head off, and a half-finished bowl of cereal and an untouched cup of black coffee, she heard her aunt making her way downstairs. Harriet straightened herself up, having thought that her aunt had left the house to tend to the horses hours ago. It appeared that she had been mistaken.

Although Harriet knew that others saw her aunt as some sort of a bullish force — bunched-up shoulders, the lack of any discernible neck, and a gravelly voice — she knew different. As her aunt entered the kitchen, dressed as she always was in her riding jacket and jodhpurs, her cheeks were bright red, and she had the vague scent of horse manure hanging about her. She smiled at Harriet. "Have an awful headache coming on." She arched an eyebrow and sighed. "Think I might've overindulged a little at Indigo Miles's last night."

"That makes a change," Harriet replied.

Aunt Adiema narrowed her eyes briefly before breaking out in a beefy grin. She waggled her finger. "You'll learn to respect your elders one of these days — perhaps then you'll stop getting the sack."

On another day, Harriet might've felt more sensitive about this comment, but given how wonderfully things were going at Humble, she was in a jubilant mood. "It's the first time I've *ever* been sacked — from anywhere. And it was after ten years. And I was actually made *redundant*."

"You say tomato, I say tomat-*oh* . . . why you didn't ever take up my offer, I'll never know." She sighed. "I suppose it's more fun when you work with your friends, isn't it?"

Harriet said nothing to this. She knew it was among one of her aunt's many Laments that Harriet had never taken a greater interest in horses. She knew her aunt — for all her constant declarations that she was delighted to never have had children — would've liked nothing more than to have a horse-mad young girl to mould in her own image, and to take on the Adiema Smith Riding School when things eventually became too much for her.

"You call that breakfast?" her aunt asked.

Harriet considered her cereal, and the black coffee. "Yes."

"What time are you off?"

"Oh, Bella said there's no meetings today — I need to pop in sometime before noon."

Her aunt sighed again. "You'll never get anywhere with a breakfast like that."

"Really, it's fine . . ."

But already her aunt was marching for the fridge, and before Harriet could raise any further protest, she had pulled open the door and was pulling things out from within.

Harriet counted out the bacon, and the sausages, and the eggs, and the tin of baked beans. "You do realise I'm coming back for dinner, don't you? I'm not going on a trip, or anything."

"Humph," was all her aunt said, busying herself now with the items she'd produced.

Harriet fully expected a silence to fall over the kitchen, and for Maximilian's purr and the gentle splattering and crackling sounds of the cooking breakfast to fill the air. However, her aunt seemed determined to continue the conversation.

"You getting on okay with those greetings cards?" she asked.

Bella sipped at her coffee. "I . . . well, my main job is to help with the customer service aspect. To help find people to buy the cards —"

"A *salesperson?*"

The way her aunt said it made the word sound like a curse.

"Uh, yeah, I suppose that's one way of putting it."

Her aunt grunted again. She busied herself with the breakfast, turning over the bacon and sausages. Harriet was quietly impressed at just how agile her aunt was in the kitchen. Most people — she was sure — believed her aunt would be all thumbs when it came to anything requiring delicate technique. She supposed that this reputation was unfairly earned from dealing with animals as large as horses all day, every day. But her aunt was more often than not kind, and delicate, even if she had sent countless little girls home crying as she berated them for some failing in their horse-riding technique.

"And she's paying you?" her aunt said, beginning to pick items off the stove, placing them onto a holding plate.

"Yes."

"How much?"

"Well, a little less than I earned in my last job. But that's just to start. I'm learning on the job, after all."

Her aunt grunted again. Although Harriet couldn't be a hundred-per-cent sure, she thought that this was a grunt of approval . . .

When her aunt finally laid out the breakfast, Harriet's stomach twisted at the sight. Her aunt stood over her, hands on hips, then said, "I'm not going anywhere till I see you wolf down the whole lot. You're far too skinny. And no matter what they say, men prefer their women to have *something* on their bones. You've to put on a little meat if you're to catch that man's eye."

Blushing, Harriet bowed her head and chomped on a piece of perfectly fried bacon, wondering just how her aunt had intuited her interest in George . . . was it that obvious?

Had she heard something on the gossip grapevine?

Some things in Normonswold never changed.

Harriet got to work a little before eleven. As she walked in through the front door of Molinaar's Cottage, she couldn't help but feel a pang of guilt. Even though Bella had *told* her to get in a little before midday, she couldn't quite shake the feeling that she was somehow doing something *wrong* . . . that work shouldn't be enjoyable . . .

that it should be a grind . . . that she shouldn't feel *happy* about what she was doing.

But there was nothing but kind smiles and greetings as Harriet entered the kitchen to find Cassandra, Bella, Robert and George, all enjoying a cup of tea. She saw that Robert's dog — Woss — was sleeping soundly in the corner.

Harriet cast a glance over the various pages which'd been strewn across the kitchen table, seeing among them sketches for new designs, graphs and tables of data, and a handful of letters with their envelopes torn and set aside. Harriet had hardly taken her place at the table before Bella had set a cup of tea of her own before her. Harriet took it with thanks, and then did her best to look focused on whatever the matter at hand happened to be — as if she might have anything of value to contribute.

Admittedly, after the first fifteen minutes or so, Harriet felt entirely out of her depth. She felt as if she was continually sinking. And, furthermore, that there was no hope of her ever being able to surface from the pit she had sunk into.

When Robert turned to her, with a kind smile, Harriet had a momentary panic. Her tongue suddenly felt too large for her mouth — too unwieldy for her to handle. It took her a second or so to match up the sound with Robert's moving lips. ". . . Don't worry about keeping up . . . you're still learning the ropes — but don't feel bad about butting in either, okay?"

Feeling a tad better about not adding anything of value to the conversation, Harriet turned her thoughts downward, onto her cup of tea. She breathed in the sweet odour, losing herself in its milkiness, in its pleasantness. She knew that the homey feeling she had warming her blood wouldn't last forever — not once she started to take on responsibility with Humble — so she decided to savour it as much as she was able.

As the meeting flowed, Harriet was surprised at how much she was able to gather about what was going on with the business. She supposed the decade she had spent at Autumn International hadn't been entirely wasted after all.

When the meeting neared its end, Harriet felt a fresh pang of panic, unsure about where things were going to go next. The others all carried their teacups to the sink, and laid them there. Not seeing anything else useful for her to do, Harriet decided to set about rinsing them out. It felt good to keep her hands busy. As if she *was* contributing something . . . even if it was just the washing up.

It was only when Harriet had set all the cups on the drying-up rack that she looked up to realise that everybody else had left the kitchen. She glanced over to Woss, seeing that he was just coming around from his slumber. Apparently noticing that his master wasn't present, he sat up, scratched himself, gave his body a quick shake, then plodded out.

There were several seconds of silence in which Harriet could hear the *tick-tick* of the kitchen clock. She felt as if her heart had synchronised with the second hand. As if the clock itself was beating out time against her throat.

Then there was the sound of approaching footsteps.

When she looked up, she saw that it was George.

Her heart skipped a beat.

"Ready for your next driving lesson?"

Harriet hesitated for a moment.

And then she nodded in reply.

8

DRIVING DESIRES

As the days went by, Harriet's burgeoning career with Humble gradually took on legs. She continued to shadow Robert as he went about meeting and greeting clients, while she kept up the driving lessons with George. This gave the two of them long stretches of time to speak. George told her all about his time in Australia — how he had ended up picking fruit so that he'd have some spending money . . . George had turned down the generous severance package Lord Charles had offered him. George had said that accepting such a large amount of money would've been nothing but a curse — it would've meant that he could do just about anything he wished. There was, at least according to George, a little wisdom in the well-worn phrase, 'Too much of a good thing'.

Harriet was surprised at how quickly she began to feel confident in George's company. She recalled the many male — and one female — instructor she had had back in her teenage years. Each of them, in turn, had become more and more frustrated with her as she failed to grasp the principles of driving. It seemed as if they took it as a personal slight that Harriet was unable to parallel park, or that she could not reverse around a corner in the approved manner.

George, on the other hand, was far more patient.

Although there was the matter of the early success of her parallel park, the feat was not so easily repeated. She had to have failed a good hundred times before she successfully managed to pull off the manoeuvre again.

And when she did, she was ecstatic.

This time, though, she had the good sense to keep her hands to herself — she was still a little ashamed of how ditsy she had acted the first time; how she had hugged George out of nowhere . . . someone of his standing and reputation must've felt as if he'd found himself cornered by some touchy, feely loose woman on the lookout for a well-heeled husband.

Because there was little doubting the fact that George *was* extraordinarily well-heeled, extraordinarily *refined*.

Harriet started to feel more and more confident in her general driving ability — that was, the way she no longer needed to consciously think about the controls as she hummed her way along country roads, braking to avoid colliding with wandering sheep, or goats, or — on one memorable occasion — an escaped horse.

There was only one really major scenario which still escaped her, and it was the one in which she had without fail fallen down on during testing:

Urban driving.

Harriet was no fool, she knew George was skilled in the dark arts of psychology; that he was working on first building up her confidence by feeding her strengths before setting her the much greater challenge of facing up to her weaknesses.

Now was the time.

Harriet had been fairly sure of what to expect when — after about forty-five minutes of familiar cruising about country lanes while they chatted about nothing at all — George told her to take a left onto the main road leading to Erma's Brook.

Although Harriet's heart beat faster, and her palms became slick with sweat, she tried not to allow any of this anxiety to show.

She was *determined* not to let the anxiety show.

She squeezed the steering wheel tightly, guiding the car into the swift-moving traffic, easing into a lane with much more grace than she had expected herself to possess. Although she didn't dare take her eyes off the road stretching out ahead, she pictured George's satisfied expression in her mind. All through their lessons together, she felt as if he had enjoyed each and every one of her successes just as much as she herself had.

Not wanting to push her luck, Harriet kept them in the slow lane on the main road. She held her distance from the lorry up ahead — George had stressed to her the importance of braking distances; of leaving a two-second gap between herself and the vehicle in front . . . and Harriet was nothing if not determined to follow George's wishes to the letter.

She wanted nothing more than to impress him.

To *please* him.

"And take the next turning on the left," George said, as the exit to Erma's Brook came up.

Harriet breathed in deeply. She again focused her mind. And although she felt herself beginning to tremble, she ignored the feeling — doing her best to counteract the blind panic which was constantly threatening to tumble in if she let down her defences for so much as a second. She pushed herself — and the car, and George — further up the slip road, and toward the approaching roundabout.

When they reached the junction, George's voice was again calm. "Straight over, and follow the signs for the town centre."

Already, Harriet was all too aware of the thickening traffic — of how cars seemed to be springing out of nowhere. And how the brake lights blinked on ahead of her.

She slowed the car.

Felt the engine rattle.

She downshifted.

The engine roared, but kept running.

She was unable to avoid casting George a brief glance. He only smiled back at her. She had the strongest urge to lean across the handbrake — to press her lips to his . . . but the traffic was moving again.

She refocused.

Brought herself back to the present.

Concentrated on following the car in front — vaguely aware that she was going along the route headed for the town centre.

The real trouble began when Harriet entered a one-way system.

Even though she had George calmly — dare she say, sweetly? — murmuring directions in her ear, she couldn't help but feel that she was facing this challenge very much alone. She and only she was responsible for herself and her passenger. Even as the thought of crashing zapped through her mind, she couldn't help but realise just how ridiculous she was being . . . how melodramatic . . . driving wasn't all that —

A horn blared behind her.

Harriet fumbled the gear stick, hitting neutral, then skipping into third, missing first entirely. The engine juddered and the car jolted to a halt. The engine ticked by for a few seconds. The horn blared again behind her. She was so glad that George wasn't saying anything right now — that he knew better than to blab away at her telling her to, 'Stay calm! Stay calm!' as if she was attempting to do anything else.

Finally, Harriet pulled on the handbrake. Found neutral. Turned the ignition. Her heart was racing when she heard the engine blaze through the car. She hit the accelerator, hearing yet another blaring horn as she leaped through a yellow-light, leaving the honker stranded as it turned to red.

As Harriet regained her composure, motoring away from the scene, she couldn't help but break out into a grin. When she glanced across at George, she saw he, too, was grinning.

"All right," he said, "that's enough road rage for one outing — let's go get some lunch."

Once Harriet had parked up in a multi-storey carpark — impressing even herself when she nailed it first time — they left George's long-suffering car behind and headed for a nearby Italian restaurant.

Harriet recalled when she had been a teenager, and a trip to Erma's Brook had always been something of an adventure. As an adult now, though, it was difficult to see exactly what charm the rather decrepit high street had possessed.

True, there were exotic locales such as tattoo parlours, and seedy-looking bars, and the odd sex shop or two . . . but when

Harriet had been younger, the place had seemed so much more dangerous. So much *edgier* . . . perhaps it was because they were visiting during the day. Maybe Erma's Brook came into its own at night.

But most likely not.

The Italian restaurant went by the name of Ravanelli's. They took a seat by the window. The place was nearly full, it being lunchtime. "Just to clear up any confusion, I'm buying," George said. "Driving like that deserves a reward."

The restaurant was decked out with white, red and black tiles. The pictures hanging on the walls depicted various sights from Italy: the Leaning Tower of Pisa, the Coliseum, the Venetian Canals. There was a small opening through which plates were passed to waiters, and through which billowed a large amount of steam. One thing was for certain, Harriet was glad she wasn't working in that kitchen . . . it looked like extremely hot work.

As the two of them sat waiting, Harriet breathed in the thick scent of onion and garlic, felt those heady odours cling to the back of her throat. She could hear the odd shout — in Italian? — as the chefs set about preparing meals.

Anticipating George was going to speak, Harriet turned back to him, sitting opposite.

"So," he said, "congratulations."

Even though Harriet knew deep down it was *silly* for her to accept any sort of congratulations just for *driving* them here, she was glad to do so. She couldn't stop herself from sending back a beaming grin. "Thanks," she replied.

"You know, you can't have had that many good teachers — that many *patient* teachers . . . it's no wonder that you didn't pass the test."

Harriet said nothing.

"Are you feeling ready? Are you feeling up to it now?"

Harriet felt a slight shiver pass through her veins. She pressed her lips together, seeing that the waiter was approaching, to take their order. When he asked her what she wanted, she realised she hadn't yet chosen, and so she went for the same thing which George had ordered: spaghetti bolognese. As they watched the waiter depart again, Harriet realised she couldn't ignore the question George had put to her.

"I don't know about passing the test," Harriet said. "I still . . . I don't know . . . it's stupid, but I feel like there's no chance of me being able to . . . like it's this impossible thing."

Sitting back in his chair, George held his head cocked to one side, soaking in everything about her stupid response. She felt like such an idiot. Why *was* he spending so much time with her? Why was he *wasting* so much of his time on trying to help her? She was a fully grown adult — surely it was time for her to act that way . . .

Finally, George gave her the flicker of a smile. "It's just confidence," he said, and then, digging through his jacket, he produced a folded-up envelope from the inside pocket. He laid it on the table between them.

Harriet stared at it.

She knew what was inside.

But, all the same, she didn't want to take it.

"It's all you from here," George said, still with a lightness to his tone of voice. "You can choose to do whatever you wish — no pressure."

9

NO PRESSURE

O n the morning of Harriet's driving exam, it seemed as if just about everything which could possibly go wrong did.

To start with, Harriet spent half the night awake, occupied with nerves, distracted by Aunt Adiema's constant coughing fits. When Harriet finally did rise from bed — already running late, and with no time to do more than thrust herself under the shower for a couple of seconds — it was only to greet her aunt down at the kitchen table, where she was wearing her very thickest of shawls, leaning over a foul-smelling, steaming bowl of what looked like leak and potato soup.

When Harriet met her aunt's expression, she flinched. Her aunt's skin had puffed up like pastry. She had turned a vague mauve colour. And she was trembling uncontrollably.

"Don't get too close, dear," her aunt said, as if Harriet had every intention of landing a great big smooch upon her lips.

Flustered, with no time to have anything resembling breakfast,

Harriet stumbled from the house, banging her head — and then her *knee* — against the doorframe as she went.

Once Harriet got out of the house, feeling her forehead and knee throbbing with pain, she made it to the Thicket Arms Inn where George was already waiting for her, standing beside his car, arms folded, looking completely unflappable . . .

Harriet thought slightly bitterly that *he* had nothing to worry about today — he didn't have to take a driving test.

She got into the car, sliding into the driver's seat, feeling as if this was the worst possible day that she had ever selected for a driving test. Even as they made it into the stream of traffic headed for Erma's Brook, and the testing centre, she was cooking up excuses for George — wanting to argue that they should turn back; that they should call up the testing centre and say that Harriet wasn't fit to drive today . . . somehow, though — and perhaps it was the nerves — Harriet managed to keep her complaints to herself.

When they reached the testing centre, and Harriet parked the car up in one of the assigned bays, she felt herself begin to tremble uncontrollably. It was as much the realisation that she had just driven the whole way through the Erma's Brook one-way system without so much as batting an eyelid as the various ailments she was carrying from this morning: the lack of sleep, the bruised head and knee.

"Need a coffee or anything?" George asked.

Harriet could only shake her head.

George nodded then looked out through the windscreen, to the grim, grey building ahead. Harriet couldn't help but think that this building — just like others like it — reminded her so clearly of Autumn International. She supposed that office block architects were in something of a hole when it came to inspiration, or maybe the whole region had got some bulk deal back when all of this had been built, decades ago.

Harriet was glad for George's steady gait, as he led her to the offices of the exam centre, and even more glad that he spoke for her; so that she needn't reveal that she was sleep-deprived along with having a — surely now visible — bruise on her forehead.

Shouldn't she tell someone she was concussed and knackered before taking the driving test? What if she crashed and killed the instructor? Would she be held accountable for her condition this morning? There was no time to think about it anymore. Was that the examiner, making her way through from the back room of the offices?

It was an overweight woman. Although Harriet wasn't in the habit of guessing people's weights, she thought she probably weighed three times what Harriet did. The woman was wearing a baggy t-shirt over a pair of well-worn jeans. She held a clipboard dangling down at her thigh, on which Harriet could see various tick boxes and spaces for the examiner to make comments . . . in less than an hour, there would be all sorts of scribbles corresponding to Harriet's driving ability, or *lack* of it . . .

George wished her good luck, giving her a wink, as he took his place in one of the waiting-room seats. He picked up one of the magazines and leafed his way through the first few pages as if he was waiting for a bus or something . . . as if George had *ever* waited for a bus in his entire life . . .

The examiner greeted Harriet, told her that her name was Sophia. Harriet gave Sophia all the information she wanted, and handed her the provisional driving licence she had possessed for what felt like her entire life. Once the examiner was done making whatever notes she had to make, Harriet got into the car, feeling — as she always did — that she didn't belong behind the steering wheel. She tried out all of the mental exercises which George had stressed to her. She attempted to remind herself that she had put in all of the practice time; that she was *competent* . . . and that she was only going to get better the more she drove. And — underneath it all — she was so aware of not letting Bella and Robert down. They had seen something in her, beyond wanting to pity her with some kind of charity in giving her a job with Humble. They genuinely believed she had something to contribute. Harriet knew passing her driving test would be the first step towards paying them back.

"Pull out and turn left, please," the examiner said, her voice steady, monotonous, but not unkind.

Harriet did as she was told, trying not to think about how clunky she felt at the controls this morning — how she wished she had got a few more hours' sleep, or that she hadn't smashed her forehead and knee into the door on the way out, and so had to contend with throbbing pain from those parts of her body.

The examiner directed Harriet about the one-way system and Harriet did exactly as she said, making sure she looked in the mirrors at the appropriate times, that she left enough time to flip on the indicators. They had been driving for about twenty minutes in the middle of town when the examiner asked Harriet to turn down one of the side streets.

Harriet squeezed the wheel tightly, feeling another jangle of pain through her knee and forehead as she did so . . . she told herself she needed to lighten up — that it was no good for her to be so *uptight* about this whole exam; yet there was always something about exams which got her uptight, which never allowed her to perform at her very best.

Harriet concentrated on leaving enough space between her and the curb on her left. She held her gaze on the middle distance, knowing the examiner would be checking to ensure she was looking in the right place — that she was aware of any and all the dangers which might be lurking down this side street.

Up ahead, there was a parked car.

The examiner told her to parallel park behind it.

It was then that something rose within her.

That she felt a sense of belief pass through her.

It pushed her onwards.

She stopped alongside the parked car, checked all of her mirrors — *signalled* — then turned the wheel, just as George had taught her, bringing them into the space behind the parked car. She had hardly given the matter much thought by the time she had straightened up the steering wheel and pulled on the handbrake, parking successfully.

As Harriet eyed the examiner out of the corner of her eye, she saw the merest flicker of a smile cross her lips. Already feeling as if she had enough confidence to say that the examiner wasn't a bitter person, she knew that the examiner had to be — therefore — *pleased* for Harriet . . . that Harriet was on the brink of *passing*. Although Harriet hadn't been in any state to glance at her watch, she instinctively knew there couldn't be much longer to go in her driving test. She had almost done it.

When the examiner told her to pull away, Harriet felt a sense of lightness overwhelming her. She had done it. She *had* done it . . . and after she had doubted herself for so long . . . after she had failed so many times . . . after —

Something — Harriet didn't have time to take stock — flurried across the road.

Harriet jammed on the brakes.

She felt herself and the examiner thrown forwards.

It was only because George had conditioned her so thoroughly that Harriet thought to plant her foot on the clutch at the same time, preventing the car from stalling during the emergency stop.

There was absolute silence.

Harriet knew exactly what the silence was saying.

That she had been *this close*, and then she had thrown it all away.

And it hadn't even been her fault!

Her heart beat long and slow. She realised she was squeezing the steering wheel more tightly than she could imagine. Her muscles were tense. And then — in one impossibly long second — she watched as a boy of about seven tentatively straightened up before the car, a football in his hands, staring big-eyed; apparently unhurt.

Harriet glared at the examiner, and the examiner — seemingly just as shocked — glared back.

As Harriet drove the examiner back towards the testing centre, she almost managed to forget she was being assessed at all. When she had seen that child stand up before the car, the football in his hands, there had been no other thought aside from the one which wanted to know whether or not the boy was okay. Once Harriet and the examiner had got out of the car, and seen that there was no damage to the boy, they had shakily bid the boy farewell, watched as he unlatched a back-garden gate and disappeared.

On the way back to the testing centre, the examiner had seemed to have forgotten her role in the assessment, too. Receiving no guidance from the examiner herself, Harriet had to use her judgement for the first few turnings before the examiner remembered she was supposed to be directing Harriet back in the direction of the testing centre.

Once Harriet had parked up in one of the bays, feeling as if she was suffering from some inescapable déjà vu — this was her *eighth* failure now — she realised there was nothing further she could do; she had given it her best possible shot.

Still somewhat pale-faced and perhaps even trembling a touch, the examiner scanned her clipboard, skimming the notes she had written. She made a few more scribbles, dropped the clipboard to her sizeable stomach, then looked Harriet in the eye.

"It's my pleasure to inform you that you have *passed*."

Harriet's mind took several seconds to absorb this — to absorb the words which'd just tumbled out from between the examiner's lips. She wondered what they might mean. She tried to tell herself she had been mistaken in what she had heard . . . was she dreaming?

When Harriet did finally reply, her own words were hardly memorable. "I . . . *passed*?"

"Congratulations," the examiner said, breaking into a toothy grin. "And, for what it's worth, that's one of the best emergency stops I've ever had the pleasure to witness. You might've saved someone's life today."

The two of them sat in silence, apparently absorbing just how close to the truth the examiner's words really were. And then — after wishing Harriet goodbye and good luck in her future endeavours — the examiner left her behind the wheel.

Harriet sat there for a long while, staring out from beneath the windscreen. Her heart was throbbing even harder now — even harder than when she had brought the car to a sudden halt before the boy who had run out into the road ahead. It was all sinking in with her. She was getting her head around what it meant; what she had *achieved* . . . and it was then she realised George was approaching . . . that he was knocking on the driver's window, grinning from ear to ear.

Feeling herself begin to shake, Harriet undid her seatbelt, allowing it to whip freely, back into the dispenser from which it came. She felt a little numb. As if all of this was playing out in some hyper-realistic dream. She opened the door, was surprised to find that her step was firm, that she didn't instantly topple over and collapse.

She drew breath.

Another.

Then she stood before him.

She felt his gentle, firm grip on her wrists.

His warm breath against her throat.

And then they just . . . moved together.

Their lips touched.

Warmth fizzled through Harriet's body — it squirmed in her gut, as if desperate to escape. She pushed it down. Deeper into herself. Determined that she wouldn't allow it to be released. She concentrated on the moment. On all that it meant to her.

She concentrated on the kiss.

10

FORK IN THE ROAD

*a*s George sped over rolling hills, he took in the City of London skyline — clear in the distance. The early-morning sunlight caught the glass buildings, giving everything a golden hue. He remembered the first time he had seen this sight and he had been brought into mind of the Wizard of Oz, and the Emerald City. Well, for what it was worth, it felt as if he had pulled back the curtain as far as it would go, and found nothing but humble humans — just like himself — flipping switches for smoke and mirrors. He supposed he should consider himself lucky to have been allowed so close to such great power; it wasn't often that someone was able to see the world through the eyes of those who owned it . . . not until they owned the world themselves; and by then it would be too late to turn down the burden which had been bestowed upon them.

His mind spun as the London skyline slipped below the horizon. He glanced across to the passenger seat where he saw his mobile phone blinking away. A new notification: text message, email . . . something like that . . . it could wait . . . and yet, even as he drove, he couldn't help wondering whether it might not be something from Harriet.

During the drive, he had tried his best to get his mind off her, flipping through radio stations. In the end, when all else had failed, he had tuned to a station specialising in football gossip — one of the many sports he abhorred — and turned the volume up as far as it would go. That had worked for maybe five or six minutes, until he had begun to get a headache, and had been forced to turn the volume down, pull in and take an aspirin with a swig from a bottle of water.

He breathed in deeply, eyeing the solid white line on his left side, recalling how he had so often advised Harriet that — when all else failed; when the road ahead had been rendered invisible for whatever reason — she could always orient herself using that white line. George certainly found himself making use of it right now, only taking the most cursory of glances up at the traffic surrounding him.

George was thankful when he reached the exit. He forced himself to loosen his shoulders, and by proxy his grip on the steering wheel. Then he realised he had something tangible to fix his thoughts on — something other than Harriet, and how radiant she had looked, and how wonderful she had smelled, and . . .

As he approached the roundabout, he realised he was going much too fast. He pumped the brakes, bringing himself to a halt only inches behind the back bumper of a white van. He berated himself silently, then got ready to set off again.

He drove on, thinking of the instructions he had been given by phone, and which he had written down and then memorised off a scrap of paper. He had been told to arrive at precisely 4.33 p.m. —

and not one minute later. It was just passed 4.15 p.m. now and he was sure he was close.

A winding road opened out before him. He was the only car now. He had left what had remained of the departed motorway traffic back on the previous main road. He switched his mind to the instructions. He was supposed to count the fields — the field *gates* — and stop at the third one. He narrowed his eyes, seeing what appeared to be the first gate sweeping into view. He drove on past it, but not without scrutinising the scenery thoroughly . . . as if he had any idea whatsoever of what he was looking for.

He drove on.

And passed another gate.

His shoulders tensed again.

Realising he had left the radio on ever so quietly, he killed it completely.

He slowed the car, feeling the hum of the vibrations passing through his bones. He had lost his headache now, and his thoughts were no longer obsessed with Harriet . . . although he was certain that was nothing more than a temporary situation.

And then he saw the gate.

The *third* gate.

He brought the car to a stop in a dirt patch in front of the gate. Then he looked around him. Glanced to the clock on his dashboard. There was still a couple of minutes. He picked up his phone to check his messages. Nothing urgent. Only a few follow-up emails he had been waiting on — confirmation of things that he had already set in place.

When he looked up again, he saw his car's dashboard clock now read 4.33 p.m. precisely. He glanced about . . . and couldn't quite help but think that he was an idiot of tremendous proportions. This had to be a joke. A *wind-up*. That much seemed certain now. This was like something out of a spy film; not out of an everyday business meeting . . . but, then again, there was very little about Kareema Ashburton which was *everyday*.

George glanced again at the clock.

4.34 p.m.

He shook his head at himself.

How could he have been so stupid?

He rested his foot on the accelerator, reached for the hand-brake, ready to push it down; to take the long journey back. He couldn't help wondering if perhaps this might've been Robert's idea of a joke — although just how he might've gone about setting such a thing up, and the fact that this seemed entirely not in keeping with Robert's sense of humour, escaped George for the time being.

"You were told to switch off your engine."

George nearly leaped out of his skin.

He twisted around. There was a young woman with hair dyed silver sitting in the back seat. It looked as if she had applied her makeup with a black permanent marker.

"I . . . I . . ."

"It's all right," the woman said. "Ms Ashburton is happy to make an exception in this case." Her expression became suddenly severe. "Although in future you shall be expected to better follow instructions. Is that clear?"

So stunned, George couldn't think of anything to say. He just found himself numbly nodding along. "Sylvie?" he asked.

She hesitated a second then gave a faint nod.

This was Sylvie, Kareema Ashburton's personal assistant — what George had been to Lord Charles.

Sylvie lifted her hand, showing that she held a remote control. To begin with, George thought that it might be some sort of laser-cutting device; that she was going to slit his throat and leave him out here, in the middle of nowhere. He had at least followed the part of the instructions he had been given over the phone which expressly forbade him from speaking about this meeting with anyone.

As his mind slowly came back to him — as he gradually got over his shock — he saw the gate ahead was now opening inwards on an automatic arm.

"Drive," Sylvie said.

Following Sylvie's guidance, George drove his way along the demarcated path swirling through the fields. When she told him to make for the barn, he had decided that there was little point in arguing. Although he had perhaps been naïve to believe so, he had thought that after his tenure under Lord Charles, there was no situation — no *reputation* or *ego* — he would be unable to handle. But he had never met Kareema Ashburton . . .

Sylvie jabbed her remote control another time and the barn doors swept open just as obediently as the field gate had done. George knew better than to double guess, or to ask for confirmation, he just drove through the gap.

Motion sensitive, fluorescent lights flickered on, illuminating the interior.

When George took in what stood before him, his foot slipped from the accelerator, and the car trundled to a halt. Right there, in the middle of the barn, he saw a helicopter.

"Come on," Sylvie said, from the back seat. "We're already running late. Kareema is not impressed by lateness." Sylvie had a slight accent he hadn't noticed previously. They had only spoken briefly over the phone, after all.

George glanced around, with half a mind on asking just where he should park the car. In the end — seeing the parking bays across the barn — he realised it would be unnecessary to ask. He pulled into one of the spaces, parked up, and killed the engine.

Sylvie said nothing, undoing her seatbelt and then getting out of the car.

George felt almost as if she was prepared to leave him behind if he was inefficient in following her lead. Just because it felt like the sensible thing to do, he slipped the keys from the ignition and dropped them in his trouser pocket.

Again, Sylvie's movements were one-hundred-per-cent efficient — without waste. She got into the other side of the helicopter and sat in the pilot's chair. She busied herself fitting a headset while George stood stunned another few seconds, trying to work out exactly what was transpiring. Sylvie shot him a fiery look and he knew he mustn't waste any more time. He was probably already on his final warning.

He got into the other side of the helicopter, fumbling his way past the wires which hung down from above like snakes from a rainforest branch. Once he had settled himself, fitted his own headset, he wondered just where they were going to go from here.

His silent question was soon answered.

Perhaps Sylvie clicked her remote control another time — maybe it was an automatic function of the barn and the helicopter's synchronicity — all that George knew was that the next thing which happened was that the roof panels of the barn slipped back and the strong morning sun shone in through the gap.

Sylvie fired up the helicopter.

Half a minute later, George found himself deafened by the

howling engine. He gripped the sides of his seat tightly. Although he had long ago left behind any fear he might've had of aeroplanes — nervous flyers would find working as Lord Charles's personal assistant a nightmare — there had always been something about helicopters which he had never quite been able to wrap his emotional mind around.

Something deep rooted in his bones which told him that there was something innately unnatural about helicopter flight.

Indeed, as Sylvie leaned on the stick and the helicopter rose up off the ground, George felt his stomach dipping down and away from him. He squeezed the sides of the seat tighter still, and looked out through the glass, straight ahead, to his car they were leaving behind.

When they had emerged from the barn, they hovered in mid-air. They were there so long George wondered if something was the matter. And then he heard Sylvie's voice over his headset. "Put this on," she said.

He looked to see what she was holding out to him.

Black fabric.

A balaclava . . . without a hole for his face.

George hesitated again. He might've been mistaken, but he was certain he heard Sylvie give a sharp intake of breath over his head-set. He took the balaclava/hood and tugged it on over his head.

If he had felt apprehensive about this helicopter flight before then he had no idea how to feel now, being unable to see anything at all. He gripped his seat as tightly as he could — as if it might plop directly out of the bottom of the helicopter should he let go.

Although he would've been perfectly happy to sit in terrified silence until they reached their destination, Sylvie finally made something resembling normal conversation. "We met at a Christmas party, did we not? Equinox House?"

"Yes," George managed to reply. "That sounds right."

"Yes, it was two years ago. You were working for Lord Charles Knightly then. That is how I came by your business card. That is how we know one another."

George supposed that — in this context — 'know' was employed in its loosest, flakiest sense, since he couldn't remember uttering more than a word of greeting to Sylvie before moving onto the next group of people with Lord Charles. To be quite honest, George didn't remember all that much about that — or very many other — parties he had attended with Lord Charles. For him, parties had been as mundane a matter as popping into the office.

"If I may speak frankly, Kareema is greatly interested in what Humble Greetings has to offer, though she wishes to meet face to face before taking things further, as is her wont."

Sylvie said nothing else.

George silently contemplated the sensation of the helicopter flopping through the air — like a perpetually stumbling horse.

About five minutes later, Sylvie said, "You can take the eye-covering off now, if you wish. Kareema likes to maintain a certain level of secrecy about her primary residence."

Wishing — as he did — to see the world again, he removed the hood. As he took in the verdant landscape, he felt his whole body tingle with something like anticipation.

It was a country house mansion.

An *extremely* fine country house mansion.

Sunlight reflected off the fountain as it pattered away, sprinkling fine droplets of water. The hedges and lawns were all so perfectly manicured that they all appeared to have been trimmed by a pair of nail scissors.

Then there was the matter of the house itself.

A manor house.

It emerged from a hill — long, modern-style windows affording a landscape view of the garden.

Sylvie brought the helicopter in around the back of the house and then down onto a helicopter pad. Her movements were so mechanical that George supposed she went through this same routine at regular intervals.

With the helicopter safely back on the ground, George allowed himself to relax, although he knew that the wait before his next helicopter flight would be all too brief.

He stared out ahead for a few seconds more, and then turned to Sylvie. "Do you have any tips for me before I meet Kareema?"

To begin with, it seemed as if Sylvie was taken off guard by the question — as if it was possible for Sylvie to be taken off guard by *anything* . . . but then, with a flutter of her eyelashes and a creeping smile, she replied, "Just tell the truth — there's nothing Kareema hates more than a *salesman*."

George held that piece of advice firmly in mind as he fell into step alongside Sylvie, the two of them making for the manor house.

PICTURE PERFECT

*H*arriet eyed the many framed designs which hung up in the front hall of Molinaar's Cottage. It was difficult to believe that Humble Greetings had only been going for a year, and that, in that time, they had already had such astonishing success. She was so proud of Bella — *impossibly* proud. And yet, there was something deeply uncomfortable, something which felt unresolved . . . and it was making Harriet greatly uneasy.

She breathed in freshly brewed coffee — a scent which seemed to be almost ever-present in Molinaar's Cottage. There was something about the smell of coffee which hung in her throat and warmed the air she breathed in. Something about it which stoked a fire in her gut and convinced her that she could do anything she wanted in this world.

She had only to act.

But then there were other times — like now — when Harriet felt bordering on despondent. When she felt as if she was nothing more than a bug caught beneath the heel of a hefty boot. Ready to be stamped on.

She wished George had been there, but he had gone to seek out someone who might well prove to be a valuable business contact for Humble; no less than the internationally renowned magnate Kareema Ashburton. She knew she couldn't begrudge George his absence — he was *working* after all — but he always had a way of making her feel more secure, more confident in herself. She knew without his personal assistance, his patience, his tenderness, she never would've had a chance in hell of passing her driving test.

And now look at her, she was a fully qualified driver; something which — ten years ago, when she had failed her test for the seventh time — she never would've dreamed possible.

When she looked away from the gorgeous, framed designs hanging in the hall, each and every one of them depicting a sweet moment between two figures, she found herself staring directly at the artist responsible. Cassandra had somehow slunk into the kitchen, and was serving herself coffee. The two of them exchanged glances and both of them gave shy smiles. Having nothing to say to one another, Cassandra had finished up pouring out her cup of coffee and was making her way out of the kitchen, apparently headed back to the studio to do some more work.

"Uh, Cass?"

Shortening Cassandra's name didn't come easily to Harriet's tongue. The truth of the matter was the two of them hadn't spoken all that much — not without being in the company of Bella or Robert. Someone to offer a foil to them. Harriet decided not to lay the blame entirely at her own feet — Cassandra was constantly locking herself away in the studio for hours at a time, working away on a design, off in her own little world.

Cassandra hung back, her cup of coffee smouldering in her hands. She smiled.

Harriet was on the brink of apologising, of somehow saying that she had been mistaken in calling out Cassandra's name, but then a sense of fortitude overtook everything, and she was determined to stand her ground. She was going to have a *conversation* with Cassandra, even if it ended up killing both of them . . .

"What are you . . . uh, up to?"

Cassandra looked at Harriet long and hard, as if trying to tease out exactly what Harriet meant by this question. "Nothing important — nothing urgent . . . just sketches."

"Oh, okay." Harriet searched her mind for something else. "I was just wondering if I could pick your . . . uh . . . brains on something?"

"Go ahead."

Harriet gestured to the table, and Cassandra took the cue, taking a seat. Harriet sat alongside her. The house was feeling quite warm and sticky, what with the humidity they'd been having this week. Harriet wondered if Bella was considering investing in any sort of air conditioning system.

"What was it like living in a big city?" Harriet asked.

Cassandra cocked her head to one side, and then glanced down at her cup of coffee. "It's . . . definitely an experience." She pursed her lips, and Harriet thought this was all she was going to get. Then Cassandra continued, "Lots of art, culture. Everything's very *vibrant.*" She glanced up at Harriet, meeting her eye. "There's always a lot going on — a lot to be inspired by."

There was a brief silence.

"What made you leave all of that behind?"

"All of what?"

"You know . . . the *art*, the *culture*, the *vibrancy*?"

When Cassandra fell into silence, Harriet was certain her instinct had been correct, that the question had been far too personal . . . at least for the relationship which the two of them shared. She wouldn't have blamed Cassandra for getting up and walking straight out of the kitchen — for simply leaving Harriet to her own thoughts.

But she finally did respond.

"Well," Cassandra replied, "despite all of the people around — despite everything that was going on . . . I felt . . . I dunno . . . *lonely.*"

The two of them reflected on this paradox in silence.

Then Harriet pushed her luck once more.

"Were your connections with other people in the city superficial? Do you think that you just didn't meet the right group of friends?"

"I . . . yeah, no . . . I'm not sure." It was only now that Harriet realised tears glittered in Cassandra's eyes. When she spoke, however, her voice was firm, unshakable. "All I can say is that it wasn't for me. It might've been the perfect opportunity for someone else. I don't know, it's just . . . everything everybody else was doing seemed — this is going to sound *really* arrogant — but it all seemed so *frivolous.*"

"In what way?"

"Nobody seemed to have any sort of an idea of how to package their work. They were all artists, undoubtedly, but not one of them really seemed interested in making it their career. They all seemed contented by the idea of having it lagging along behind them like some sort of a hobby. Well, that's just not for me, I'm afraid. I don't know if I'm a less authentic artist than most, but I've always wanted to make a living from what I love: from my art. Everything else is a waste of time."

The tears were still in Cassandra's eyes, but her tone was more resilient than ever. As if to underline what she had just said, she wiped her eyes with her shirt sleeve.

Harriet allowed the silence to flow and grow between them again, and then she said, "I was never even brave enough to leave my home town. I think anybody who goes out into the Big Bad World deserves an awful lot of credit. I never even really tried."

Cassandra looked Harriet in the eye, the flicker of a smile settling on the corner of her mouth. She put her coffee cup to her lips and drained what remained of its contents. When she set the mug down, she said, "I think we should put the kettle back on."

Harriet couldn't quite believe that she was having *this* conversation with Cassandra. It was the conversation which she had always told herself she would have with Bella one day, when she got around to it . . . and yet the conversation had never happened.

So she was having it with Cassandra now.

With a fresh cup of coffee warming her hands, she turned her thoughts entirely to what lay within her. What had been trapped inside her chest for so many years.

"In some ways, I felt like me and Bella were twin sisters growing up. We did everything together. We were best friends, but we never argued like other friends did. I never imagined we would drift apart . . . until we did. The two of us were planning on moving together to London — doing just what you did . . . until that plan fell through."

Harriet said nothing more. She was certain that Cassandra could more than fill in the gaps of just what had been the catalyst for Harriet and Bella's falling-apart — that Harriet had stumbled across her father kissing Bella on the doorstep of Ebbendevor, Bella's family home. Things like that just never stayed secret in small towns, and the first thing that any outsider arriving to Normonswold would receive — after the standard welcome hamper from the Village Council — was a brief, but thorough, rundown of the town gossip for the past several decades, if not *centuries.*

Harriet gathered herself. "When Bella did go to the big city, I felt that everybody looked at me with a sort of pity, as if I had been the one who had been left behind, and — I have to confess — that's exactly how it felt to me . . . I did feel as if I was the one who had been left out. Not permitted to enter that whole interesting adult world."

Harriet expected Cassandra to leap in with some comment or other, but she didn't. Harriet was pleasantly surprised. Whenever she had attempted to have this conversation with her Aunt Adiema, or with Dorothy, she had been interrupted . . . been told in different ways that she was 'master of her own fate' . . . except she didn't feel she was . . .

"We were going to share a flat in London," Harriet went on. "That was how we planned it. You have no idea how hard it was to see Bella come home — Christmas after *Christmas* — and to over-hear all her stories of just how she was getting on in the Big City. All of the exclusive parties she was attending. The cool, creative job she had landed. It felt as if she was living in a whole different world, while I had the obligation of popping just down the road to the offices there. And all the dynamism that entailed."

Still, Cassandra said nothing.

Harriet parted her lips to speak again, but realised she had nothing left to say. She had no idea what Cassandra might be thinking about her now — if she indeed thought that Harriet was self-centred and jealous. Perhaps she was wondering how to bring up this conversation with Bella later on . . . to warn her off this supposed 'childhood friend' who she had ushered into the fold of her heart project.

But then Cassandra spoke.

"I've found, when I go home, there are people from my childhood who are still around — who are living in more or less the same places, working in more or less the same jobs, seeing more or less the same people."

Harriet felt her heart sink slightly, believing Cassandra was dragging her down the same road all of the others had. She prepared herself for the lecture — for all that *carpe diem* bullshit.

"But," Cassandra went on, "those people were all . . . *happy* about where they ended up. They had no intention of doing anything else." She shrugged. "Oh, sure, some of them *talked* about how they would maybe like to go and live somewhere else — about how the grass was greener over at this place, or that place — but it was always obvious they would never actually get themselves up and move *anywhere*." Cassandra drew breath, stared down into her coffee cup. "I think there comes a point when — everything else aside — people have to be responsible for their actions. There's nothing to be gained by wondering what could've been, or anything like that . . . there's only the present moment . . ."

As Harriet sat at the table, feeling her body throbbing with the rush of caffeine from the two cups of coffee she'd drunk, she was unsure just whether Cassandra hadn't said what she had expected, albeit in a completely different way to how she'd heard it before.

But Cassandra wasn't quite finished.

"It's not about *doing* something about the future; it's about making peace with your past . . . once you've done that, once you're free of whatever burdens you've laden yourself with, you can work out what it is that you really want."

"I have a confession to make," Harriet said, then glanced up briefly at Cassandra. "That is, if you hadn't already heard. I'm only here because I got fired from my job — I feel that, if it hadn't happened, I would've been there another ten, twenty . . . thirty years."

Cassandra nodded along. "And how does that make you feel?"

"I . . . don't know . . . some part of me feels appalled that I spent so much time doing something that I clearly cared very little for, but another part of me — and this is some weird, bundled-up mixture of the emotional and the logical — says that I never really wanted to move away from Normonswold. This place has and always will be a part of me. Safe and secure. And I like that — that's what I've always wanted, I suppose. I mean, after all that happened between me and Bella, after the whole falling-out . . . losing the most important person in the world to me, Normonswold was all I had left. All I had to rebuild my life around." Harriet smiled widely. "But that doesn't mean Aunt Adiema's going to have the final word on me taking over her riding stables."

The two of them laughed.

12

PARTY AT NOON

*W*hen Harriet finally surfaced from her bed — the sunlight beaming through the gap in her curtains and streaking across her eyes — she felt a strange, positive energy bound through her. There was something which told her that today everything was going to go well; that today everything was going to be *perfect* . . . that she was going to finish the day much happier than she had started it.

Across the room, hanging from the wardrobe, was the grass-green dress she had picked out for Indigo Miles's Midsummer Party — a staple in the Normonswold calendar, and attended by anyone who was anyone in the village.

As Harriet ran her hands through her hair, looking at her complexion in the mirror and wondering what she was going to do with her makeup, she felt Maximilian twist about her bare calves, purring his head off — no doubt looking for food.

She scooped him into her arms. Although he was reluctant at first — scrabbling to get free — she eventually convinced him otherwise, caressing his tummy and bringing out his throbbing, seemingly never-ending purrs.

Once Harriet had had her fill of fuzzy, she let Maximilian free, and he promptly skipped out through the bedroom door.

She stretched her shoulders wide, looked to her dress again, and then felt herself beginning to smile — wide and bright.

Harriet turned up on the doorstep of Ebbendevor — the Miles' family home — at high noon. Aunt Adiema stood at her elbow, breathing heavily — as she seemed to do more and more these days following even the lightest of walks. After much deliberation with Harriet, she had finally gone with a pale purple number, coupled with a ruby broach depicting a horse's head. Harriet remembered back when she had been a teenager, and she had gone to visit her aunt, she had always believed she was so *silly* to always be wearing something or other to do with a horse. It was only now — in adulthood — that she realised just how important it was for someone to be able to identify themselves with *something*.

What did Harriet identify herself by?

It strained her to think about it.

There was Bella with her writing. And there was Cassandra with her illustration. And then there was Robert with his straight-laced, no-nonsense logic to set the world to rights. Finally, there was George with his winning charisma and patience. Held up to those people, Harriet felt as if she was just blowing in the wind, looking for somewhere to land.

Where would she end up?

As always, Indigo Miles's Midsummer Party was packed to the rafters. Indigo had spared no expense when it had come to the arrangements. There were waiters seemingly sliding out of nothingness, all of them bearing trays fully packed with flutes of champagne, tumblers of whisky, and glasses of white wine. Then there were the hors d'oeuvres, but Harriet didn't feel like she had much of an appetite. She just wanted to stand a while, and not say anything to anybody, to just be whisked along by her aunt's firm grip.

The faces all blurred together, the other invitees. Some of them — *most of them* — she recognised. She had seen them at all of the Midsummer Parties she had attended in the past. And she had seen them throughout the entirety of her life in Normonswold. They were people who seemed in some fashion to be anchored to the deep recesses of her subconscious. Impossible to shake free from her memory even if she'd wanted to.

And then she saw him.

It was as if the crowd parted to reveal him to her.

George.

He was dressed in much the same way as the other men — in a light-toned summer suit. But there was something about his eyes, and she could see it even at twenty paces. The way that they twinkled. When he turned his gaze onto her, it made her feel as if she was the most important person in the world to him. Or maybe she was just inventing it.

Trying to fool herself.

Wasn't that the thing with lust?

Didn't it drive you wild, play tricks on you, and then leave you looking like a fool?

Sure, he had been kind to her, and he had been patient too . . . and they had kissed . . . but what made her think she was any different to the — no doubt — endless others who had preceded her. And then she stopped thinking because just the thought of him being taken away from her — finding comfort in the arms of another — turned her stomach.

George shook off the person he was speaking to with marked aplomb. She knew these were the sorts of social skills that weren't taught anywhere — that *couldn't* be taught by being told . . . they were picked up from thousands of hours of practice in being in this or that upper circle. It warmed her heart to see him approaching, and to know that he had cut away from his conversation just so he could come over to her.

That he could attend to her needs.

Harriet breathed in deeply, and felt her aunt's hold on her forearm slacken, and then release. She didn't look back to her retreating aunt — glad Aunt Adiema had seen sense, and decided to leave Harriet and George be.

There were some things only another woman could understand.

As George closed in on her, it felt as if there was something in the air. It was something which drew her in, which enveloped her body, swallowing her entirely. It was both parts fear and anticipation which told her that he could do anything — *anything at all* — that he wished with her. He had only to say the words. He had only to show her the way.

He reached out and laid his hand against her cheek.

She felt the warmth of his touch.

Blood surged to her brain.

And she knew that she was his.

"Oh my goodness! I must say that I haven't got around to *congratulating* you, Harriet, dear! Well done — *very* well done!"

A little startled, Harriet turned in her chair. Off in her own little world, sat beside George at one of the many tables arranged on the lawn, she had somehow hardly heard Indigo Miles's extremely loud approach. Some people had compared Indigo Miles's tone of voice to a foghorn, others had chattered about how she was like a bull in a china shop . . . Harriet had always thought she was more like a town crier, complete with the clanging bell; the constant search and distribution of gossip being her prime motivator.

Today, Indigo had gone with a floaty, white summer dress. A golden necklace dangled from her pale throat, and she wore the daintiest of dainty watches about her wrist . . . its strap gold, too, of course.

Dorothy was standing beside her. He was wearing a shimmering purple dress which seemed to be decorated with fish scales, though it was beyond Harriet's remit to call into question Dorothy's taste when it was almost without a doubt on another planet to her own.

"Not so much as a *card!*" Indigo shrieked. "Goodness me, I do hope that you *will* forgive." Indigo glanced about, as if she was deeply worried that someone might be looking on with a seething look of disapproval, and then she closed on the pair of them as if to impart a secret. To her credit, she did drop her voice to about half the volume of what it had been previously. That said, Harriet still would have been able to hear Indigo's voice from the front gate of the house. "I *do* have something for you . . . if you will promise to be *just a little* patient." She tapped the bridge of her nose, and then straightened up, bringing her tone of voice back to the level to which everyone was accustomed. "A toast!" she called to the crowd.

Instantly, the invitees turned away from their conversations.

A smattering raised their glasses, and then the rest followed.

Soon enough, everybody's eyes were fixed upon Indigo Miles . . . all apart from a boy and girl, in their early twenties, chattering away to themselves, backs turned. All it took to turn them around was Indigo clearing her throat. They instantly spun around, the two of them giving cowed expressions, thoroughly ashamed to have challenged her authority.

Harriet thought that the red-haired girl was very pretty. She couldn't recall having seen her previously. Not around Normonswold. Perhaps she was from out of town.

"I wish to mark this day as one of celebration, in the name of Harriet Tumblebeach, for her noble achievement of passing her driving test." Indigo tilted her head to one side. "It might well be true to say that she has taken her good *time*."

Here Indigo slipped Harriet a wink — and whereas anybody else hanging her out so enthusiastically in public might've caused her great discomfort — Harriet couldn't find it within herself to feel badly towards Indigo.

Indigo Miles was a force of nature.

To put it mildly.

"All the same," Indigo continued, "we *must* celebrate her and wish her well on her journey. A new-born sense of freedom."

There was a long pause.

Almost uncomfortable.

If Harriet hadn't known Indigo so well, then she might've thought she had just made a spectacle of herself. But the winning smile reappeared. Indigo held up her glass then tilted it back down her throat, and her invitees erupted into applause and cries of "Hear! Hear!" led by none other than Dorothy.

As with all of Indigo's Midsummer Parties, the intensity didn't let up for a moment. And it was entirely down to the efforts of Indigo Miles herself. It was a marvel to observe, how the waiters and waitresses became an extension of herself . . . how she managed to be so entertaining, and to hold conversations with everyone, and yet never lose sight of the party as a whole. Harriet wished she could say she was watching and learning from Indigo's example, but the truth of the matter was that she — like everyone else — was struggling to keep up. Everything was so flawless, and so subtle.

Even as the sunlight faded, and the waiters and waitresses lit candles, tastefully arranged throughout the back garden, Harriet was surprised to find she felt no tiredness . . . she felt nothing but rampant energy to just *keep going* . . .

As she sat on the fringe of a conversation George was having with an elderly couple from Brighton — telling them at length, and in a much more fascinating manner than Harriet could ever have expected, about their generations' old fishery business — she noticed Bella and Robert approaching. She saw, out of the corner of her eye, that Bella was stuck in the middle of a wide yawn, and that Robert too — somewhat unusually for him — had deep, dark bags hanging from his eyes. The two of them, though, when they got closer, were smiling contentedly. Bella waited until the wife had reached the end of the current hilarious anecdote about a live haddock which'd somehow found its way into their bed, then turned her attention onto Harriet and George.

"Don't feel compelled to stay longer than you want to," Bella said, in a hushed voice. "Mum won't be offended if you want to slip away, all right?" She looked to Robert. "We're going to turn in." She shook her head. "I just don't know where she finds the energy. I'd say that she saves up all her energy the whole year for this occasion, but then there's no explanation for how she acts the rest of the time."

Robert smiled, then eyed Bella. "Your mother would make a fortune in events management, in the city."

Bella looked back at Harriet. Rolled her eyes. "We all *know* that money will never be a factor in any of my mother's decisions."

Harriet looked to George. "We're doing fine, anyway, aren't we?" She studied him for any sign of fatigue, and if there was something to be extracted from his expression, then she well and truly missed it. Perhaps she needed more experience — more *training* — in how to read people. Or perhaps George had learned to hide his true feelings expertly.

George looked to Harriet, and then to the elderly couple. Finally, he turned back to Robert and Bella, gave a shrug and a pout, then said, "Your loss — Midsummer comes but once a year."

Bella smirked back. "Trust me, I appreciate that better than you could know." She cracked a smile, once more casting a glance over the whole group. "Have a good night!"

"Sleep well," Harriet said to Bella and Robert as they departed.

Robert's dog Woss lagged at their heels as they left the party, clearly looking forward to the early night ahead of him.

13

AFTER HOURS

*A*s the night went on, and invitees slowly began to dribble away from the party, Harriet thought that she was going to feel the same sense of fatigue — that she was going to feel, as she always did, the urge to be by herself for a period of time.

But not tonight.

True enough, a dew settled over the back lawn, and a chill carried on the breeze. But this only meant that the remaining guests made their way indoors, to shelter in the welcoming heat of Ebbendevor. In the end, those who remained at the party found their way to what Indigo Miles termed the Piano Room.

The Piano Room wasn't called so without good reason. Framed pictures of various antique pianos, of sheet music, and of black-and-white photographs of past concerts hung from the walls. Once the drapes were pulled, the whole scene felt impossibly cosy. She thought of all the times when she and Bella had spoken about leaving Normonswold behind forever, and how Harriet had found it difficult to believe — *even back then* — that anyone could ever want to leave a home like Ebbendevor. Then again, Harriet's home had long ago disappeared. She had nowhere left to go. She lived in a house with her aunt, and her cat Maximilian, but it would never feel like *Harriet's* home.

Dorothy took his place at the namesake of the room — the grand piano around which were arranged armchairs, and sofas, and poufs. He slipped the hem of his dress up ever so slightly and then took his seat on the bench, his surprisingly dainty fingers resting upon the keys and then beginning to play. He kept the music quiet, the soft pedal dampening the piano, accommodating conversation.

Just as he had been throughout the evening, George was infinitely entertaining with the other guests. Harriet watched on from his side as he enraptured them in his stories of the Australian Outback, and how he related his many entertaining anecdotes about his time under Lord Charles's employment. Whenever he reached a dramatic pause in the current story he was telling — a wide smile pressed onto his lips — he would slip Harriet a conspiratorial glance. And she would feel herself warming from the inside out.

As he continued to hold the whole of the Piano Room enthralled with his endless tales, Harriet couldn't help but notice the red-haired girl she had seen outside. The red-haired girl sat close to the boy she had been with earlier. There was something distant about the couple now, though. She saw how the boy lightly laid his hand on her side while the girl seemed entirely oblivious of the gesture.

When the whole of the Piano Room erupted into laughter following George's latest witticism, Harriet surreptitiously got up and sat down near the girl. She did her best to catch the girl's eye. But she was unwilling to meet Harriet's gaze.

Harriet allowed herself another few seconds, for George to begin telling another story, and then she leaned over and whispered in the girl's ear. "Do you want to talk?"

The girl's reaction was immediate. She straightened up so quickly that it was as if someone held live wires to each of her big toes. She looked to Harriet again, her eyes wide, and then, without a word to her, got up and shifted off across the room.

A tightness squeezed Harriet's chest. The boy stared at her with ire . . . as if it was Harriet's fault for the girl reacting in such a violent manner. Harriet was afraid of the boy getting up to follow. But when she got up, walked across the Piano Room, the boy made no attempt at pursuit. He remained where he was — pinned down by George's latest story.

Outside the Piano Room, Ebbendevor was quiet.

Harriet felt a draught creeping about her exposed calves. She felt the cool stone against the soles of her bare feet — by way of common courtesy, she had ditched her heels on the back porch before setting foot in the house.

She moved on quickly, all her senses coming alive. It was as if some animal nature guided her on the trail of the girl. She knew instinctively she had made her way into the kitchen, and that was the way that she went.

Harriet had half expected the kitchen to be something of a disaster zone. Indigo Miles *had* just put on a party for a hundred or so people, after all. But it seemed that Indigo had had the foresight to see to such *issues*, and the kitchen was entirely spotless. Harriet felt a pang of pity for whichever members of the waiting staff had

had to stay behind to return the kitchen to such a pristine state. Then her attention darted to the girl.

She sat by one of the windows, a cheek pressed up against the glass.

As Harriet approached, she couldn't help noticing that the garden too was completely neat and tidy. There was no suggestion that there had been so much as a single person out there all evening. Harriet thought back about what Robert had said about Indigo being capable of making a killing at events management, and she wondered just how much of an understatement that really was. If only Harriet could discover her own talent so easily.

The girl glanced around to Harriet.

Their eyes crossed.

Harriet's heart thumped in her throat.

She breathed in deeply.

Told herself to be calm.

To *exude* calm.

She settled in the seat opposite. "Hi," she said, not knowing where else to start.

After a slight pause, the girl replied. "Hi."

"Are you, uh, friends with Indigo?"

"My family is, yeah. But they couldn't come. I'm kind of representing them all here." She smiled slightly. "The flagbearer, or whatever."

Harriet smiled back. "What's your name?"

"Jeanie."

"Is that your boyfriend, back in the Piano Room?"

Jeanie nodded.

"Look, I don't want to pry, or anything, but are things okay with him?"

Jeanie got halfway through nodding again, and then she simply broke down.

Harriet was so taken off guard by the sudden reaction, that she was unsure how to deal with the situation right away. And then her female sense kicked in.

She shot up out of her seat, rounding the table.

She wrapped her arms about Jeanie's shoulders.

After a moment's hesitation, when Jeanie resisted her, she began to trust, leaning back into Harriet. The two of them remained like that for the longest time. It felt like an hour or more, but it might just as easily have been two or three minutes.

When Harriet sensed that it was the moment to speak, that the girl would be receptive to what she had to say, she asked, "What's on your mind?"

"I . . . it's just . . . I don't know . . . everything seems to be happening so quickly." She gently prised herself away from Harriet. The air in the kitchen was sticky, moist. "I finished university this summer, and . . . well . . . the next step is for me and . . . and Daniel — my boyfriend — to move in together . . . he's taken care of everything . . . he's . . . I don't have anything to complain about really . . . it's just there's no time to think . . . no time for me to work out exactly . . . exactly . . . what it is that I want . . ."

"And what do you want?"

"I . . . don't know . . . I mean, I know that it sounds stupid, like I'm just a little girl . . . but I think I want to stay here . . . I want to stay in Normonswold. I . . . my family's here.

Harriet said nothing at first. She allowed Jeanie's words to die away in the kitchen. And then she said, "Have you spoken with . . . Daniel about this?"

Jeanie shook her head. "I . . . don't want to worry him . . . it's not fair on him . . . he has worked so hard to make things work for us. To accommodate the two of us. It would be unfair for me to stand in the way. For me to . . . to . . . *ruin* all his planning."

Harriet breathed in again, and then she looked out to the garden once more. "You know," she said, "there was a time when I thought that to achieve anything in my life, I would have to leave Normonswold behind — I would need to leave my family and friends *behind* . . . but, I don't know, I don't think I believe that much anymore. You can do more than you could ever imagine in your home town. Things don't have to be like they have always been. You don't need to leave forever to change completely."

Jeanie stared at Harriet long and hard. "I just . . . I don't think that I want to take the next step . . . and I'm just not sure . . . not sure that it involves me moving away . . . not forever."

Even though Harriet thought she and Jeanie had struck up a confidence between the two of them without much trouble, she was apprehensive about asking the next question. She decided there was really nothing to lose — and perhaps something to gain. "Do you love him?" she asked.

Jeanie thought about this a moment. And then she nodded. "Yes," she said.

"Okay," Harriet replied. "Then maybe you're going to have to compromise. You're going to have to work out what's really important to each of you. Work out where you stand. Do you think you could tell him what you've told me?"

Jeanie scrunched up her expression. She breathed in deeply. For a moment or so, Harriet didn't think she was going to respond at all. "I . . . don't know."

"It's something you should think about." Harriet reached out for Jeanie's hand, took hold of it with her own. "Your needs are important too — just as important as his. But you have to make him aware of them, otherwise he will never do anything at all. He will never understand what's wrong. You need to *spell it out* to him."

Even as Harriet uttered the words, she wasn't entirely sure just where all this wisdom was flowing from. After a few moments, she convinced herself that it was most likely from Indigo Miles or Aunt Adiema.

They sat together in silence for a long while. There seemed to be nothing else left to say. Harriet, at least from her perspective, felt that she had given Jeanie her best shot.

A few minutes later, there was the sound of footsteps out in the hallway. The two of them turned to look. Standing in the doorway was Jeanie's boyfriend — Daniel. Although Harriet had had the vague notion that he might be somewhat angry that someone had sequestered his girlfriend, on the contrary he smiled gently at them both.

"Uh, Jeans? Do you want to get going?"

Jeanie looked to Harriet, and Harriet nodded back at her.

Without another word to one another, Jeanie got up and left the kitchen with Daniel.

For the longest time, Harriet continued to look out into the hallway, to where Jeanie had departed. As she listened to the front door open and then close with a *thud* — the car engine start in the near distance — she wondered how things would go for Jeanie.

If she hadn't created a monster.

14

ON THE LINE

George held his phone pressed to his ear, looking out of his window at the Thicket Arms Inn to the street outside. Normonswold certainly lent itself to summer — there was an undoubtable glimmering, golden quality to the village when the sun peeped out from behind the clouds. He watched people shuffling their way up and down the street: dogs, children, parents and grandparents; it really was a Most Whole-some Scene.

"Hello?"

George snapped back to the phone — to the voice on the other line. "Hello? This is George — George Meltz."

"I know who this is."

Kareema Ashburton's assistant, Sylvie, was — as ever — impos-sibly cool-sounding. She made him believe exactly what she said. If she had told him that she was psychic, that she could picture him perfectly in the room in which he was currently standing, then he would've been apt to believe her. Even though George knew he must stay calm — that it would serve nothing to get riled about things — he felt himself begin to sweat.

Perhaps it was the stifling weather outside.

"You were supposed to wait for our call, George."

"I . . . know," George replied. "It's just that it's been a while . . . and I just wanted to check that things were . . . that they were *ticking* along."

There was a long pause on the other end of the line, and George tried to picture Sylvie . . . and utterly failed. She might just as easily have been behind the wheel of a car, or propped up casually at the controls of a stationary helicopter, or — like him — standing by a window and admiring the beautiful summer's day taking place outside.

After a while, he pulled the phone away from his ear, believing Sylvie had hung up. But he saw that the call was still active. That he hadn't been given the brush off quite yet.

"As a matter of fact," Sylvie continued, "Kareema had planned on giving you a call in the near future. She was . . . *impressed* by what you had to offer. She believes that it lends itself to . . . *scalability*."

George was perplexed for several seconds. He had almost forgotten what they were talking about. And then it returned to him in a single, crunching realisation:

Humble.

This was about Humble Greetings.

"All right," George replied, and then, forcing a smile, knowing that this would make his voice sound brighter, friendlier, on the other end of the line, "How should we go forward?"

"In one week, Kareema requests your presence at her Scottish residence. She would like you to bring a selection of representative samples, along with your ideas on the marketability for the product internationally." Sylvie paused almost reverentially. "Does that fit in with your plans?"

George was caught on the hop. And then he remembered himself. "Yes," he replied. "Yes, of course . . . that's completely fine."

"Good. We shall look forward to welcoming you at Broidersbarth."

With that, the phone went dead.

George continued to stand at the window, looking down at the passing world outside. He realised he was trembling, and he told himself that it was with good cause. There were not many things more nerve-racking than a private sit-down with Kareema Ashburton — especially when you were trying to sell her something.

Or so he had been told.

15

ROAD TRIP

*H*arriet felt She was caught up in a daze as she sat in on the meeting at Humble Greetings. The meeting was on the topic of — as it had been throughout the entire last week — Kareema Ashburton. Even though Harriet had known next to nothing about Kareema Ashburton before the beginning of this week, George had quickly brought her up to speed, explaining at length about how so many of the products she used every day only *existed* because Kareema had given the say-so for them to stretch their legs in the international market, and so given them the resources to dominate on a domestic level.

As always at Humble, the meeting took place around the kitchen table. Harriet felt the warm, gently breathing form of Woss pressed up against her shins, out of sight beneath the table. For some reason, he had decided she was the most comfortable human to sleep against. Maybe it was because she wasn't moving abruptly and without warning — like the others arranged about the table.

Perhaps it was because she was sitting still and silent while the others all seemed to be losing their minds.

This was supposed to be the final meeting before they ventured north to go and stay with Kareema in her Scottish residency . . . or *Broidersbarth,* as George had told her it was named. They were meant to have a good idea of how they were going to approach the meeting — tactically speaking — but even to Harriet's inexpert eye, it looked as if chaos reigned supreme. This was the closest she had seen George to losing his temper. Robert, conversely, remained as calm as ever; as seemingly unshaken, while Bella and Cassandra looked on anxiously. Harriet felt much better when she caught either of the girl's eyes and felt a warmth deep down in her gut to feel that they were on her wavelength . . . that they were just as beleaguered by all this talk of people in high places who could influence the future of Humble Greetings with nothing more than a snap of the fingers.

As George finished his latest speech, about the importance of them all being briefed on the exact 'strategic goals' of Humble over the course of the next five years, it was Bella who held up her hand to quiet any further discussion.

"Look," Bella said, "I think we should all just pack up and go. We've talked about this enough. We work for Humble and its goals every single day. I don't think we could be any more prepared. It could be that we pull this off, or it might be that we simply don't have what Kareema is looking for. I think we need to make peace with that now."

There was a host of doubtful glances, mostly passing between Robert and George.

Harriet just turned her attention downwards, onto Woss sleeping at her feet.

Nobody was saying anything, so Harriet decided it would be her to break the silence. "Shall we just 'pack up and go', then?" She continued to stare at Woss's handsome flanks for another few moments before turning her attention upwards, seeing that everyone was focused upon her for once. She felt herself flush slightly.

"Yes," Bella replied, her voice a touch raspy. "Let's get going."

They decided on taking two cars for the trip up to Scotland — Cassandra would ride along with Robert and Bella, while Harriet would go with George.

As Harriet rounded George's car, preparing to stoop down into the passenger seat, he told her to stop, and — grinning for what felt like the first time in weeks — told her that they would be taking the driving in turns. Harriet felt a slight lurch in her gut, but supposed it was only fair that she do her part of the driving now that she was fully qualified . . . now that George had invested so much of his time in *training* her.

Although they had spoken at length about the possibility of taking a plane up to Scotland, it had been decided that it would be much quicker — more efficient — for them to make the eight-hour-or-so drive. By the time they got to the airport on time, cleared security, took off, landed, located a hire car, they might just as well have driven.

All the same, despite this practical argument, Harriet couldn't help but feel a tingle of fear. This would be — by some distance — the longest drive she had ever made . . . albeit with a support driver for company.

As Harriet sat behind the wheel, she watched Robert helping Woss into the boot of his car. Robert then gave Harriet a thumbs-up and got into the driver's side. Without any further warning, Harriet heard him start up the engine and watched on as he pulled away from the side of the road.

Harriet looked to George, as if she still required him to tell her how to use the controls. Then she squeezed the wheel, turned the ignition, and set her sights on the road ahead.

The early morning soon gave way to a full-blooded summer sun. As Harriet joined the motorway, following along at a regular pace behind Robert, she felt a strange sense of confidence flooding through her — a great, reassuring sense of wellbeing.

She breathed in deeply and told herself to keep her eyes fixed on the road ahead, and not to sneak off too many glances in George's direction; to where he was busily working away on his laptop. That was far easier to think than to put into practice . . .

Around lunchtime, they pulled into a simple burger place where they wasted no time at all in eating. There was a sense of urgency about what they were doing. As if Kareema Ashburton herself might somehow be watching them — already keeping track and making judgements on just how much of a professional outfit they really were.

After lunch, George took over the driving, and Harriet was glad to stretch herself out in the passenger seat for a while. Although it sounded a weird thing to say, sitting down and turning a wheel every so often — making minor adjustments with the pedals — was actually quite an exhausting business. She turned her thoughts to the scenery blurring past, enjoying the sight of summer — if not the sound or the smell — before beginning to feel guilty when she turned her attention onto George's closed laptop sitting in the back seat. She supposed George had far more pressing business to attend to than gently guiding the car along a seemingly unending stretch of road. He was the one who would truly matter in the meeting with Kareema Ashburton, after all.

And so, after they had stopped to take an afternoon tea, Harriet volunteered to take over the driving from George — and although he protested briefly, she insisted. Once they started driving again, George contentedly continued to tip-tap away at his laptop keyboard.

Harriet had to admit that she felt a flush of panic when — six or seven hours into the journey — she saw Robert ahead of her making to turn off the motorway. She glanced to George, still absorbed by his laptop screen. Seemingly sensing Harriet was a touch distressed, he looked to her, smiled, and then nodded.

That was all the encouragement she needed.

<hr />

The roads became long and winding. Harriet did her best to stay alert. She realised she had gone tense — over her entire body — and that she was now clinging to the steering wheel as if her entire life depended on it.

It was now that she felt George's gentle touch on her forearm.

When she looked to him, she saw he had closed his laptop, laid it down at his feet, and that his whole attention was upon her. "Loosen yourself up, a little bit. Just *relax*."

But even with George's calming voice, and the reassuring guidance of Robert driving ahead, Harriet couldn't help but feel she was on the cusp of losing control; that she might end up driving into one of the grassy verges which'd sprung up on either side of the road.

She made a point of relaxing her shoulders, preventing herself from tensing up entirely, and she somehow guided the car along the countryside lanes without coming to trouble.

About half an hour off the motorway, George gave her a direction which gave her great cause for concern.

"Overtake Robert."

Harriet looked to the road rolling out ahead, and then to Robert, who she saw had now pulled into one side of the road. She allowed the car to slow down. When it rolled to a stop beside Robert, she glanced across at George. "What'd you say?"

George was busy with his mobile phone. "You need to overtake," he repeated.

Harriet remained where she was, parked up against the grassy verge, and then — checking her mirrors, as she had been instructed throughout the many driving lessons George had given her, she saw there was nobody around and she pulled out and around Robert's parked car. She felt strange to have George in the passenger seat beside her, pressing the phone against his ear, while she left Robert behind at the side of the road. She felt almost as if she was some sort of a solitary explorer — mapping for the first time this region of Deepest, Darkest Scotland.

George began to speak with the person on the other end . . . well, if speaking could be said to constitute the occasional, "Yeah," or "Uh-huh", here and there. He continued to hold his phone to his ear, and Harriet wondered if he had forgotten all about her. With no further instruction, she followed the road ahead. When she checked her mirrors, she saw Robert had started to trawl along in their wake.

It was about ten minutes of George holding his phone to his ear, and Harriet guiding the car on through the countryside, before George — without warning — reached out for the steering wheel and gave it a hard tug. He sent the car careening to the left.

A bolt shot up Harriet's spine. She felt a flash of anger and panic. When she somehow wrestled back control, preventing them from toppling into a ditch at the side of the road, she realised they were now heading up a steep dirt path. If she had seen the route on any other occasion, she would have thought it was a footpath. But she trusted George's judgement. He still said nothing to her, continuing to listen in on the phone pressed to the side of his skull. Not even a mumbled apology for so sudden a gesture.

As Harriet examined the rear-view mirror, she saw the dust rising up at the back of the car. It was difficult to make out Robert, Bella and Cassandra following behind. She wondered if they were still there. If the sudden manoeuvre George had performed hadn't been some trick to shake them off the trail . . . though whyever George would want to shake them off escaped Harriet.

Harriet's deliberations only came to an end when she had to turn her full concentration to the matter of climbing a steep slope. She went through her mental checklist, balancing the accelerator, picking the right gear, getting herself into the correct road position.

When they reached the top of the slope, Harriet prepared herself for a sudden drop downwards — again picking her mind for the training George had imparted to her. Before so much as a thought could scoot through her brain, however, George hammered his fist on the dashboard. A second or so later, Harriet pumped the brakes, following the driving instructors' universal signal for emergency stop.

With a crunch as the car slid across the dirt path, she brought them to a halt.

Her heart pattered against her ribcage as she awaited George's next order. But he remained unmoved, the phone still pressed to his ear.

Finally, he spoke to the person on the other end. "Okay. We're here — in position."

Harriet turned in her seat, seeing that Robert, Bella and Cassandra were making steady progress up the hill behind them. She imagined stopping on the side of a hill, and starting again, would present little challenge to an accomplished driver such as Robert.

She looked around, seeing the greenery, the copses of trees, and the steep valleys. She could tell that they were at the highest point for miles around. She wondered if there might be a monolith, or similar, to mark this, but from just looking around she couldn't see one.

From somewhere, a low-grade *hum* commenced.

And then it gave way to an unstoppable *roar*.

When she looked in the rear-view mirror, she saw an object occupying everything.

Blocking out the sunshine.

Harriet's whole body locked up.

She gripped the steering wheel as tightly as she could.

She slipped George a glance, looking for an explanation.

For the first time in what felt like forever, he turned to her — the phone still pressed to his ear — a look of panic on his face.

Harriet fumbled with the handbrake, deciding that now was the time to get them off the high ground. That if she didn't act quickly then they were going to collide with whatever was behind them. When Harriet tried to start the car, she stalled almost instantly. Somehow she found the will to calm herself so that she might try again.

But it was in vain.

As swift as she was in getting the car started again, and in preparing to drive them down the hill and out of danger, she was too late.

16

THE CASTLE

*D*espite the pleasantly cool glass of red wine in her hand, Harriet was shaking. She was still shaking, just as she had been half an hour ago when she had arrived here.

She looked around her, to the stone blocks which formed the walls, to the tapestries which hung down around them, and to the suit of armour which stood sentry at her bedroom door. There were half a dozen windows in the room, though none of them were much bigger than the size of her head. When she looked out through them, she caught snatches of the castle grounds, of beautifully kept hedgerows, of a loch stretching out between fanned-out valleys, and the reams of blue sky, soaring off into the unknowable distance.

The lighting in her bedroom — in what she had been *told* was her 'bedroom' — was warm and modern. Indeed, aside from the period details, the interior of the castle seemed to have been decked out with all the mod cons. Everything that a person needed for survival in the twenty-first century.

Still, it was difficult to get rid of the idea completely that she wasn't a prisoner here. And the fact that she was being held in solitary confinement hardly helped matters.

She looked behind her, to the four-poster bed, and then to the double doors which she hadn't previously noticed. They were well worked into the general décor of the castle — painted a noble burgundy. She thought of going exploring before thinking better of it.

To tell the truth, she was scared stiff.

Harriet took another sip of her wine, tasting the familiar flavour of something between old boots and plastic. That was always how it tasted at first, as the palate got used to it. She couldn't doubt that the liquid warmed her from the inside out, though.

And *God*, how she needed warming right about now.

Even to think about how it had happened sent chills up her spine. How she had been ready to pull away, to drive her and George down the hill, away from the castle, and to safety. But, as Harriet had jammed her foot down on the accelerator, the sound of the car engine lost to the much greater noise of whatever machinery had flopped through the air overhead, she had soon realised that she no longer had control. And that — what was more — they weren't heading downwards.

They were going *up*.

It was the shock, more than anything, which had led to Harriet engaging the accelerator even harder, and it had only been George's calming voice which'd managed to get through to her, to assure her she could switch off the car.

While she had been alone here, she had thought about his tone of voice often.

If he had come across as at all demanding — if he had tried to *scare* her into doing what he wanted — then she was certain that she would've panicked all the more, and that she would never have had the sense to switch off the car engine. As it was, though, she had obeyed him; and once she had switched off the engine they had floated along beneath what had turned out to be an enormous helicopter; a well-behaved, tame passenger.

It was as they had drifted in over the latest breath-taking loch that George had told her to prepare for landing. Harriet had had another panic in wondering just what exactly she was supposed to do to prepare. And then she realised that she needed to release the handbrake; that was about as far as common sense got her.

Their host had trundled them down to a gravel stretch. Harriet had gripped the steering wheel as she had felt the car tyres making contact with solid ground. Something detached itself from the car roof and she had allowed herself to exhale as the helicopter chopped off into the distance. She had sat stiff at the wheel, watching as it took off in the direction they had come, apparently going to collect Robert, Bella and Cassandra.

Harriet and George couldn't have landed more than a second before several men and women — all of them dressed in the unmistakeable black and white of waiting staff — had materialised all around the car. They had turned their backs to them, looking out at the surrounding area, as if they were some form of an armed escort . . . as if their bodies might be able to block them from stray bullets. It was then that Harriet realised the ground was sinking. It was only when something slid shut above their heads, and artificial lights blinked on to reveal their surroundings, that she realised they were now in something which had to be an underground car park. There were countless cars all parked up in countless bays. Harriet had never been sufficiently interested in cars to know exactly what the makes and models were . . . but she knew enough to know that there were more than any one person could possibly need.

When the platform bringing them underground had ground to a halt, one of the members of the waiting staff had rapped his knuckles against the driver's window — near enough scaring Harriet out of her skin — and politely requested that she step out of the car. It being George's car, Harriet had glanced to him for approval; not wanting to be held responsible later for giving up his vehicle to carjackers — albeit extraordinarily polite ones.

Once they had stepped out, Harriet had experienced the strange sensation of being surrounded by the waiting staff. And though, more than anything, she had wanted to be *close* to George, the people surrounding her were intent on them gradually being separated.

Before Harriet could do anything further, she felt her arms gently but firmly seized, while George was taken hold of in a similar manner. She had time to see him disappear through an exit on the other side of the underground carpark, while she went through another.

And, next thing she had known, after a whirlwind trip through several castle corridors, and up more than one winding staircase, she had been delivered to this room here — abruptly left, albeit with this glass of cool red wine.

She took one more sip, then, deciding that perhaps she should be more circumspect about what she was eating and drinking, she set the glass down on a wooden chest.

She looked to the double doors which seemed to lead to an adjoining room and decided the time was right for her to explore. However, she had hardly got to her feet when there was a brief knock on her bedroom door.

A female member of the waiting staff appeared. She bore a

white towel, and a shimmering, golden dress on a coat hanger. She smiled.

Feeling somewhat beleaguered, Harriet took the towel and dress from the woman, although she was unsure what to do with herself once she had done so.

"I shall be back in half an hour to take you to dinner," the woman said.

Harriet watched on as the woman left her bedchamber. Once she heard the door thunk shut, she turned to the double doors, took a deep breath, and then pushed her way inside.

The bathroom was all that could've been expected from the hospitality of the castle. The whole place was covered in black and white tiles, and there was a stonking, enormous bathtub with protruding feet in the form of dragon claws. The bath might come in use later on, but Harriet knew that for the time being — for the purposes of this evening — the shower better suited her. She needed to get ready for dinner.

The shower was located across the bathroom, and the shower-head itself emerged from the wall where it would splash down onto a surface designed to catch the run-off.

Harriet undressed and then turned on the tap, surprised to find that the water was pleasantly warm already. Although she couldn't say she had ever previously stayed in a castle, one of her over-riding presumptions would've been that the plumbing was stuck somewhere around the seventeenth century in terms of innovation . . . not so here.

Once she got herself clean — using the kindly supplied array of soaps and shampoos beside the shower — and dry — courtesy of the white towel she had been provided — she put on the golden dress she had been given, only noticing now that she had been given no matching footwear. And the dress hardly suited putting her trainers back on. In the end, she decided to go barefoot . . . that seemed to be the only sensible option.

Harriet had hardly brought the dress down over her head when the female member of the waiting staff returned. She felt a pang of suspicion, wondering if she was being watched somehow.

How had the woman known so easily that Harriet would be ready?

Harriet was almost entirely certain that the trip up through the castle had the sole purpose of disorientating her. She felt her head begin to spin as she struggled to keep up with the waiter. They climbed higher and into the castle, feeling the not unpleasant sensation of her bare feet against the cool, worn-down stone slabs. Harriet reached the point where she was certain there couldn't be much left for them to climb.

When they finally reached their destination — about five minutes, and seemingly countless staircases later — Harriet found herself emerging onto the castle turrets.

The platform was expansive and offered a vista of the entire grounds.

There were no other buildings in sight . . . only rolling hills and valleys, and lochs set in the moonlight which streamed down from the clear night sky.

She expected it to be chilly up here, so was surprised that it was pleasantly warm. The feeling up on top of the Scottish castle had more in common with somewhere in the tropics than somewhere in the Highlands.

She couldn't help but wonder if Kareema Ashburton had some

technological wizardry ticking away in the background to cater for such a sensation.

It took Harriet a couple of seconds absorbing the view before she realised there were others on the rooftop with her. Other members of the waiting staff. And — her heart beat quickly as she realised it — a table set with a white tablecloth and illuminated by candlelight.

Harriet was the first one here, and she wondered just why she had been bestowed this dubious honour. It was then she realised there was someone sitting at the head of the table. Harriet approached, seeing in the dim light that the woman had dyed silver hair, and that she drew attention to her already distinct features with stark, black makeup.

"Hello?" Harriet said.

Currently busying herself with some handheld device or other, the woman took about half a minute to finish what she was doing, and then glanced up. She gave a distant smile. "Good evening, Harriet. My name is Sylvie. I am Kareema's personal assistant." Returning to her handheld device she added, "Please, take a seat."

Harriet looked to the table, to each individual place. There were six of them. She held back for several moments, not really sure what to do. Then she decided to take one of the places furthest away from Sylvie. She had no intention of sitting at the other end of the table so she would need to make eye contact with Sylvie once Sylvie had inevitably finished her business with the mobile device.

In any case, as it turned out, Harriet wasn't to be alone for long.

She watched on as Cassandra — looking as confused as Harriet felt — emerged onto the roof. She wore a dress in the same style as Harriet, albeit sapphire rather than gold. Like Harriet, she was barefoot. Cassandra was soon followed by Robert and Bella —

Bella wearing a ruby-red dress and Robert in a silk, white shirt over a pair of loose-fitting grey trousers. They, too, were barefoot.

Although Harriet gave each of them kind smiles of greeting, she couldn't shake her attention from the stairwell leading back down into the castle, wondering just when George was going to appear. In a moment of panic, she wondered if they hadn't been kidnapped by some cartoonish forces of evil, and George had sided with the Baddies . . . as it was, though, she had no need to worry.

Dressed in the same manner as Robert, George emerged with his own personal escort. He met Harriet's eyes briefly, and Harriet felt something akin to a spark tickle the inside of her chest. George took his seat at the head of the table.

Once they were all sat down and waiting, Harriet turned her attention onto Sylvie, who was still fiddling with her handheld device. She wondered if she was being pointedly rude, or if she was genuinely as busy as she seemed to be. In any case, not one of them thought to make conversation while they waited.

When Sylvie *was* finally finished, she looked over the whole table with a smile spreading her cheeks. It was as if she had invited them all here — *old friends* — so that they might share some kind of joyful reunion. "Thank you *so* much for making it," Sylvie said. "It really means the world to Kareema that you were able to attend personally."

Although nobody said it, the open observation about this particular comment was if Kareema *indeed* valued their presence in *her* castle then why wouldn't she be here to greet them all personally?

Harriet, though, knew it wasn't her place to say anything.

She was just here to learn what she could.

And to keep her mouth shut wherever possible.

She had no intention of being the one to ruin this for Bella, or for Humble.

"So," Sylvie continued, without the slightest trace of discomfort at having to make awkward conversation, "how was the journey here?"

There were general mumblings of contentment.

"Good, good," Sylvie replied smiling widely. Then she straightened out her expression somewhat. "Kareema does *severely* regret being unable to attend you this evening — something has come up, as I hope you will understand. With any luck, she will find her schedule more accommodating tomorrow. In the meantime, however, I would encourage you to enjoy all that the castle has to offer. Please wander as you wish — leave no stone unturned!" It was now that Harriet realised Sylvie was getting up from the table; that she was leaving them already, without having eaten anything. "And *do* enjoy your dinner, won't you? Kareema personally oversees the kitchens — she really does want her guests to have the best cuisine that is on offer."

And, with that, she rose and left.

There was a long silence, and only the vague sound of a breeze blowing through distant valleys to break it. And then one of the members of the waiting staff stepped forward to take their orders for the evening.

17

NIGHT-TIME PROWLERS

*A*lthough Harriet had interpreted Sylvie's claim that they could wander the castle at will as something of a courtesy, than as an invitation, the others appeared to think differently. Once they had finished with their dinner on the castle turrets — Harriet had elected the Mediterranean Salad, followed up with a bowl of chocolate ice cream — they descended as one down the staircases, led by Robert and Bella.

To be quite honest, their trip of exploration was borne more out of necessity than a true sense of nosiness since there was no member of the waiting staff to guide them back to their chambers.

The first room they came to had been fitted with an enormous, panoramic window which offered a view almost as good as the one from the rooftop. Harriet supposed that Kareema used this particular function room when the Scottish winter took a firm hold of the landscape and rendered going up to the roof a non-prospect.

Within the room, there was a collection of sofas, and tables with chairs gathered around. There was an unattended bar against one wall.

Once they were finished with that particular room — still with Bella and Robert leading the charge — they continued to explore the castle.

Next time around, they somehow stumbled upon the Armoury.

As Harriet trod over the threshold, she felt a skittish sensation in her stomach, as if she was violating some childhood taboo. As if her parents were going to come careening through the door at any moment to tell her off . . . as ridiculous as *that* sounded even inside her own head.

As its name suggested, the Armoury contained a whole array of weaponry — broad swords, crossbows, maces, as well as helmets, chest plates and other assorted defensive kit. Some of the items were displayed hanging from the walls, while suits of armour were stood up on mounts, putting Harriet in mind of all those films about haunted castles from her youth where said suits of armour would get up and walk around.

Once they had tired of the Armoury — which was well over forty-five minutes after they had arrived — they left through another door. As they went along the passageway, Bella announced that they had somehow stumbled upon her and Robert's bedroom.

After wishing them a very good night, Cassandra, George and Harriet stumbled on through the castle, doing their best to make some sense of their surroundings.

Harriet couldn't help but sneak the odd glance at George, convinced he did really know where he was going, and that he was — for some reason — dragging them about on some sort of a lark. It was impossible to convince herself that George was ever confused about anything.

After another ten minutes of walking, Cassandra informed them that they had reached her room, and she bid them goodnight.

Harriet wasn't sure what got into her, but she felt her cheeks flush slightly as she pecked a kiss onto each of Cassandra's cheeks and then watched her disappear behind the chamber door. As she headed on through the castle, she felt George reach down and take hold of her hand gently. She felt more confident now — like she could do anything at all she put her mind to.

It felt as though they walked the castle corridors for hours, as if they had entered some sort of inescapable maze. But, with that precise thought on her mind, she suddenly recognised a spiral staircase to her left. Such was her surprise and excitement, that she released George's hand, breaking away from him to explore.

Sure enough, she had taken no more than a few steps up the staircase when she realised she had arrived. Her bedchamber. She glanced back over her shoulder, seeing George there. He was smiling gently. "Would you like to . . . come in for a minute?"

George nodded.

Harriet felt her stomach twist slightly.

Blood rushed to her head.

She fumbled the bedroom doorknob, but finally got them inside.

Since she had been away, somebody had been into her bedchamber. There was now a jug of water and a trio of spotless tumblers to drink from. She looked around at George, seeing that he too was taking in her bedchamber.

His gaze shifted onto the door adjoining the bedroom. "What's through here?"

"The bathroom."

George looked to her and then opened the door.

Harriet secretly wondered just what he was trying to prove —

if he wanted to confirm that she was telling the truth or something. Whatever his motivation, it was undeniable that there was a bathroom on the other side of the double doors.

Harriet followed on George's heels.

"Well," George said. "That's interesting."

"What? Why?"

George just gave her another of his smiles then trod on into the bathroom, going to a door on the other side which Harriet hadn't previously noticed. Once he opened the door, she realised there was another bedroom on the other side.

And then she felt a skitter of fear down her spine.

She had undressed and washed herself in the bathroom, completely oblivious that she shared this space with another person. Her whole body locked up and she held her breath.

George inspected the bedroom before them, looking at the four-poster bed, and then turning his attention to the window which looked out across the rolling hills and bottomless loch illuminated in the moonlight. Then he turned back to her — still smiling. "My bedroom," he said.

It was nothing more than the slightest of quivers, but she noticed it in his voice. It was only then that she realised he was feeling just as shaken as she was by the notion that he had been unwittingly sharing his bathroom with someone else.

Now, though — now that she knew for a fact it was George — there was another feeling which flooded through her. And it was becoming increasingly difficult to control.

When she locked eyes with him, she did her best to put her thoughts and emotions into words. But then she realised it was hopeless. That there was only one way in which she could truly express herself in any kind of satisfactory manner.

She lurched into him, catching him off-guard.

It felt sweet to make him uneasy . . . if only for a moment.

She reached up and dug her fingernails into his muscular shoulders.

And pressed her lips up against his.

It was the element of surprise — certainly not her slight weight — that caused George to almost lose his balance; to send the both of them toppling over.

In the end, George caught himself — he caught them *both* — against the castle wall.

Harriet held on as tightly as she had done in the first instance. And she felt her hands — almost apart from her realm of control now — make their way down George's body, an unstoppable exploring force. She untucked his dress shirt, and fumbled the button on his trousers. Before she had really taken stock of just what she was doing, she had him down to his underwear. And panting.

A shudder passed across the length of Harriet's skin.

Her heart pumped more quickly.

She seized hold of George once again, feeling for the first time she was the one in control. That she was the one dictating the pace. She thought of all the times when he had been the expert — when he had taught her how to drive; how he was effortless in the company of business people; and how he was seemingly unshaken by any given situation.

Well, now she had caught *him* off-guard.

George tried to recover, to reach out for her dress, no doubt wanting the two of them to be on equal terms.

Not yet.

She was determined to draw this out.

She was enjoying her sense of control.

She was enjoying being the expert.

She pressed herself harder against George, feeling his relaxed muscles, and the sudden twitches just beneath the surface of his skin as his inner-being implored him to take back control. But he had lost control now.

She had the upper hand.

Feeling as if her own body had caught fire, she led him by the hand to the four-poster bed. She gave him a push, dropping him down on the mattress, before climbing on.

Standing up, feeling as though she towered above him, she drew the curtains on the four-poster bed feeling an impossibly deep sense of power over him with each movement.

She had him cornered.

Trapped.

He was hers and hers alone.

She got down on all fours, placing one of her knees on either side of his body, and she finally allowed his hands to explore. But on her own terms.

She guided his hands up her smooth lower back, and then to the arches of her shoulders. All the time, she felt him easing up the golden dress she had worn for the evening. She no longer had the urge to play with him any longer. She was happy to allow him to take her in.

To *lust* for her.

She viewed him through the narrow slits of her eyes.

There was something about these surroundings which set something almost . . . *evil* within her. Something which brought out an impish impulse.

And she quite liked it.

As he reached for the waistband of her underwear, she held out a hand and stopped his progress. With a smile, she looked down at his own underwear — which was still very much present around his waist.

"You first," she said.

In the moonlight which snuck in through an opening in the four-poster curtains, she saw the smirk lining George's lips. She had to restrain the urge to throw herself upon him another time — to press their lips together once more.

To *regain* control.

But as she reached down to remove her own underwear, she realised that the power games — if that was what they had been — really didn't matter any longer.

They were together now.

A single item.

And it was with this thought, that she reached out and shut the crack in the four-poster's curtains. Sealing them in together.

And blocking the world out.

18

BREAKFAST IN BED

*W*hen George finally came around, he could feel the sun shining. Even through the thick curtains which surrounded the four-poster bed, he felt the glow of its rays warming his blood, bringing his mind back awake, preparing him for the day ahead. And yet, even despite these natural biological functions, he failed almost entirely to find the will to return to the waking world.

He turned to look across the bed, to the sight which appeared to be unfurling from some kind of dream. Harriet sleeping there, her golden hair — so much like the tone of the dress she had worn the night before — spread out across her pillow.

Gently, so as not to wake her, George propped his shoulders against the headboard. He took a moment to gather himself, and then he slipped silently out of the sheets.

Upon discovering the dressing gown, and the accompanying slippers, he was somewhat taken off-guard — taken off-guard by the knowledge that neither of these items had been present the previous evening, when he had arrived here with Harriet. It meant that someone had placed them there during the course of the night. Even though George had spent enough time in the upper echelons of power to know that house staff were often afforded more trust than a bank manager, it still felt like an unnatural order of events to allow others into your private world — to give them free passage into your *bedroom*.

Any sense of anger or resentment at the invasion — if that was really what it was — soon dissipated. Although it was true to say that George had never been the quick-to-anger type, he found it especially difficult to sustain any sense of ire this morning.

There really was no reason for it.

George shrugged the dressing gown on around his shoulders, and slipped his feet into the slippers. As he silently made his way out of the bedchamber, he couldn't help wondering just why Kareema Ashburn — or whoever was in charge of such decisions — had decided he should be granted footwear this morning.

Last night they had been made to go barefoot . . .

As he slipped out of his bedchamber, leaving Harriet behind, sleeping, there was no conscious thought about where he was headed — about what he was trying to achieve by leaving the prospect of a lie-in behind. It was only when he came across a male member of the house staff, carrying a covered silver tray that the thought struck him.

"Good morning," George said.

"Morning, sir," the man responded, speaking in a thick Scottish brogue.

"May I?"

The man looked uneasy for a moment. Then, with a vague smile, he relented, handing the tray to George. As George thanked the man and turned away, he couldn't help but feel his gaze upon him, as if he was afraid that the moment George escaped his sight, he was going to do something ignoble with the breakfast tray, such as toss it down a flight of spiral stairs, or maybe out of one of the castle windows. Perhaps the man had a catalogue of experiences to share when it came to uncouth guests . . . maybe there had been more than a few wild parties in the time during which the man had served here.

When George returned to the bedchamber, he felt as if his feet were lighter, despite the extra burden of the breakfast tray. He looked out across the beautiful, verdant landscape, the sun glimmering in the sky and beaming its warming rays all over.

He laid the silver tray down on the bedside table and then — concentrating on being as gentle, as careful, as he could manage — he reached for the curtain of the four-poster and drew it back to reveal Harriet sleeping soundly within.

Gently, he sat down on the edge of the mattress. He studied Harriet's delicate features; her China-doll mouth, and the natural reddish tint to her cheeks. As he watched her, he felt the shift in her breathing — she took shallower and shallower breaths. And then, with no discernible movement, she opened her eyes.

"Morning," George said.

"Morning."

George realised he was grinning so widely that his cheek muscles were beginning to ache. And yet he could seemingly do nothing to stop himself.

Thankfully, Harriet was smiling back . . . that made him feel less like a grinning weirdo. "Last night was," Harriet began, but was cut off by a knock at the door.

The two of them looked around, to the entrance.

After a moment, George's senses returned. "Come in," he said.

A female member of the house staff slunk into the bedchamber.

She had a mousy aspect, as if she had been hiding out in one of the nooks or crannies of the castle, waiting for the appropriate moment to pop up.

"Ms Ashburton shall see you this morning at ten o'clock." She glanced about the bedchamber and then — no doubt comprehending that she was intruding — swiftly left.

George looked to Harriet and felt himself plunge deeper into her eyes. For the best part of the last six months he had been working at achieving a private meeting with Kareema Ashburton. The goal had occupied his every conscious thought.

Now, though, he realised he wanted nothing more than to shut the curtains, bolt the door to the bedchamber, and stay here with Harriet.

Pretending that the rest of the world simply didn't exist.

19

BREAKFAST BUSINESS

eeling the warm water stream through her hair, and down her cheeks, Harriet's only intention was to get herself ready as quickly as possible. She knew she really had next to nothing to contribute to the team about to meet Kareema Ashburton, but she was determined she wouldn't let them down. She wouldn't keep them waiting or look as if she didn't fit in with the rest. She wanted nothing but success for Humble.

When she left the bathroom and returned to her own bedchamber, she found clothes awaiting her, spread out across the bed she hadn't used the night before.

There was an emerald blouse, and a pair of smart, well-cut trousers.

Once again, there was no sign of any shoes, but after the previous night's excursion through the castle, she had learned that shoes really weren't all that essential.

Harriet dressed and then left her bedroom behind. She looked about the corridor, somehow getting it into her head that everybody would be waiting for her there — she had simply assumed that she would be holding everybody else up. However, when she took a few steps down the corridor leading away from her bedroom, she was glad to see that this wasn't the case at all.

A little way along, she emerged into an antechamber which she recognised from the night before. It was from here that she noted various doorways leading down a series of corridors, and realised that this must be the common link between all their bedrooms.

She took a seat on one of the comfortable sofas and settled in to wait for the others.

Bella and Robert were the first to emerge, and then Cassandra appeared a minute or so later. It must've been the first time in her life that Harriet had seen Robert looking nervous. Like the night before, he was wearing a white shirt over a pair of smart black trousers. He seemed unable to leave his shirt cuffs alone, constantly picking at the buttons as if he wanted to remove a troublesome loose thread.

Beyond a morning greeting, they said nothing else to one another, all of them — barefooted like Harriet — looking on to the corridor which led to George's bedroom.

Another minute passed.

And another.

Harriet's heartbeat quickened. She couldn't help but wonder if George wasn't caught in some kind of panic. If he wasn't currently undergoing some sort of a breakdown. Perhaps he had reached the limit of his powers — maybe his confidence had only been able to operate until a certain point.

And then she heard footsteps.

Harriet exchanged glances with Cassandra, and then Bella.

She knew the same thoughts skittered through their minds too.

Only when George trotted into view did Harriet allow herself to believe that he was really okay — that he had really come to join them.

George's uneasy expression didn't shift from his face, despite Harriet mustering a nervous smile and meeting his eye. He turned his attention onto Robert, and said, "The laptop — I don't have the *laptop.*"

Unable to keep herself from witnessing the encounter, Harriet found herself looking at Robert, studying his reaction to this comment. Even if it was true that Robert was feeling somewhat nervous at the prospect of meeting Kareema Ashburton, he managed to keep a straight-faced expression. He didn't so much as blink.

"Okay," Robert replied, then looked to Bella. He put on an unconvincing smile. "Let's get going, shall we?"

Harriet looked to George, but he refused to meet her eye. Perhaps he thought of himself as a failure for misplacing the laptop, but it cut her much deeper than that.

With a nod, George took off along the corridor, taking the lead, and the rest of them followed.

Just how George knew which way they were supposed to go remained a mystery to Harriet. Although — as they proceeded along the corridor away from the antechamber leading to their bedrooms — she believed that she was coming closer to fathoming the logic of the castle. It no longer seemed mysterious and impossible to understand how the house staff could navigate these twisting, turning corridors without the aid of a map.

George brought them to a pair of double doors which'd already been thrown open — apparently in anticipation of their arrival.

There were two members of the house staff standing at either side; their expressions neutral, waiting to serve.

George murmured a morning greeting, and then glanced back over his shoulder as if suspecting that the others had deserted him; that they had lost whatever confidence they had placed in him since he had failed to bring along the laptop.

The room before them was compact — with a table set for no more than six — but it didn't seem that way what with the windows which occupied all three walls, affording yet more devastatingly beautiful views of the surrounding area.

Harriet had to force her attention back onto the table before her. There was silver cutlery all laid out. Placemats. Covered dishes. Glasses for orange juice. Mugs for coffee. She looked to the others as they found their places and realised she should look for her own.

While George took up a chair at the opposite end, Harriet found herself sitting beside Cassandra, next to the empty seat at the head of the table. She looked to Robert and Bella, seeing the beginnings of concern on their faces. Harriet was readying herself to stand and propose that maybe Bella should change places with her — so that she could sit beside Kareema Ashburton — but the sound of footsteps approaching made this impossible.

The person who appeared in the doorway was not Kareema Ashburton, but her assistant from the previous night, Sylvie.

Eyes fixed on the device in her hands, she acknowledged them with a wave before taking up a place in one of the chairs arranged around the table. It made Harriet slightly uneasy to feel that there was someone sat behind her, but she did her best to put the thought out of her mind. She knew she was hardly an important cog in these talks, and that her role was to keep her mouth shut and not say anything stupid.

There was a silence for about a minute, and then more footsteps.

Harriet glanced to Sylvie, as if she might offer them some clue about how they were supposed to act in Kareema's presence, but she remained glued to the device before her.

Like the others, she waited for Kareema to appear.

Harriet's relative sense of calm surprised her — how she only felt the very faintest tickle of her heart beating against the underside of her throat. She had thought she would be nothing but a bag of nerves at this point, but she had somehow managed to maintain control.

Kareema appeared to *float* in through the doorway. It took Harriet a while to realise that this effect was caused not by something mysterious, but by the fact that she wore a long, flowing, azure robe which trailed on the ground behind her.

Harriet took stock of Kareema's face, her slightly chubby cheeks; her lush, full, shiny white hair. She might have been in her sixties, or in her nineties. It was impossible to tell. If she had chosen to dye her hair then she might've appeared even younger still.

Kareema wore a permanent half-smile; one of those expressions which made Harriet think that the person wanted to communicate the idea that despite being slow to anger, it was best not to push one's luck.

Harriet felt as if she was back in school as she found herself getting to her feet and reciting — with the others — "Good morning, Ms Ashburton."

Kareema smiled back, then ushered them into their seats.

Harriet nearly tripped over her chair legs as she sat back down.

Waiters appeared soundlessly all around.

Sitting at Kareema's elbow, Harriet felt terribly exposed. She consoled herself with the fact that because Kareema was busy giving her own order to one of the waiters she would most likely not have time to notice Harriet giving hers.

Harriet asked for scrambled eggs, toast, and for coffee rather than tea. Orders taken, the waiters left the table, and the whole room descended into total silence once more. All of them were staring at Kareema, who now spoke for the first time.

"I must thank you all for making the time, for going *so far* out of your way, to come and meet with me." She paused as if she was expecting some form of protest — as if one of them was going to claim that driving all the way up to the middle of nowhere in Scotland hadn't been 'going out of their way'.

Nobody said anything.

Kareema glanced across the table, looking directly at George. "I have already had the fortune of meeting Mr Meltz, here, several weeks before, in preparation for this meeting, and although I imagine he has already told you enough about me so that you might know how I operate, I think it might be best for me to spell these terms out again so that there might be no confusion in the matter."

Harriet glanced across the table to George, seeing he was flushing slightly. Then she looked to Robert and Bella, realising the two of them were also looking at George.

Although George had certainly said nothing to Harriet, she was surprised to gather he had seemingly said nothing to Robert or Bella, either. Then again, perhaps George hadn't believed whatever Kareema had had to tell him was of any importance. That it was merely additional detail. Kareema, though, clearly had other ideas.

"I don't believe in contracts — I don't believe in a lot of *traditional* business practices."

Harriet could almost *hear* Robert's toes curl upon hearing this.

Kareema continued, "There are those who think me foolish — *and very numerous they are* — but I make it my life's work to cut my own path, to make my own decisions, to stick to my own sense of values. My own particular purpose." She looked about the table as if expecting one of them to oppose this.

When Harriet glanced to Robert, she saw he was staring back at Kareema intently. She couldn't help imagining that he might be biting his tongue. If there was anything in the world which Robert abhorred it was a lack of organisation. He was one of those people who believed that rules existed for a reason, and that reason was to keep the world from chaos.

For the first time, Kareema's mouth creased with a smile. "Now that I have explained myself a little, perhaps you would like to tell me more about your venture?"

20

THE PERSONAL CONNECTION

*B*ella spoke almost nonstop as Harriet picked and nibbled at the eggs, and toast, and rashers of bacon that the waiting staff brought out to them. Harriet did her best to keep up with Bella's constant flow of ideas and thoughts concerning Humble, only looking occasionally to Kareema to see whether or not any of this information was sinking in.

Harriet wondered just what Kareema had exactly meant in her speech — how far exactly the idea of 'renouncing traditional business practices' stretched.

As Harriet sat at the table, listening to Bella's outpouring, she sensed that Bella was close to tears several times as she explained her thoughts and motivations in creating Humble Greetings; just what the mission statement for the company truly meant . . .

While Bella spoke, the waiting staff returned to clear the plates, and to top up their cups of coffee. Kareema listened attentively to what Bella had to say for over an hour before holding up her hand.

At the rate she had been going, Harriet wondered if Bella would've continued to nightfall without this prompt to stop.

"Thank you very much for that summary," Kareema said, smiling widely. "Most informative, clear, and honest." She glanced across the breakfast room for the first time to Sylvie. Harriet noticed that Sylvie was no longer staring fixedly at her mobile device; that she looked ready to perform whatever action Kareema wished.

Kareema dismissed Sylvie with a simple nod.

Then Kareema turned in her seat and stared directly at Harriet.

This brought Harriet's train of thought to an abrupt halt.

To begin with, Harriet looked over her shoulder, truly believing that there was someone else behind her who had caught her attention. Seeing there was no one there, however, she turned back.

Kareema smiled easily at her. "What do you think about Humble?"

Harriet felt a twitch at the base of her stomach. She looked to the others, expecting someone to break in and to correct Kareema, to tell her that Harriet had just started with them, that she knew next to nothing about the business.

But nobody said anything.

And Kareema continued to stare long and hard at her, waiting.

Harriet snatched a breath, her mind doing flips to try and find something appropriate to say. And then she decided she just had to do her best. "I . . . think it's wonderful." Harriet felt a lump form in her throat and looked around the table, again hoping that some-body might be able to bail her out of this uncomfortable conversation.

She just *knew* that she would be responsible for Humble not making the right connection with Kareema Ashburton.

She did her best to calm herself, then went on, "The cards have proved very popular." She forced a slight smile then looked to Bella and Cassandra. "Bella is a talented writer, and Cassandra's illustrations are just . . . well, *wonderful* . . ." She allowed her words to trail off, hoping Kareema would cotton onto the idea that she had nothing at all useful to say about Humble. And although Kareema did speak, it was not what she had expected her to say.

"Let me explain myself," Kareema replied, glancing up at the rest of the table. "I like to think that after all these years doing, well, whatever it is that I *do*, I have become quite adept at reading the dynamics of any given team. I find it easy to identify — just from a single glance — the hierarchy."

It surprised Harriet to see that Robert was nodding in accord with what Kareema was saying this time. And there she was, expecting he would've been just as appalled as when Kareema had renounced everything Robert knew and loved.

"I like to hear from everybody, and it has been my experience that it is often best to speak with the lowest members of the hierarchy before gradually working my way upwards — so that those members will not feel intimidated about contradicting what one of the higher-level members might have said . . . I have always followed this strategy." She looked again at Harriet. "You are Humble's newest employee, are you not?"

Harriet nodded.

"It has been my experience that every employee has something valuable to contribute towards their perspective of a business to those outside of it — everybody has a unique point of view, a different angle on things." She smiled more widely at Harriet. "If you please, would you outline what you see in Humble's future?"

Harriet did the best she could to speak about all she had thus far seen at Humble. Before she had begun to speak, she told herself she shouldn't go into depth about areas she knew nothing about — that she should simply stick to the few business meetings she had sat in on with Robert and George, and the general administration she had been helping with at Molinaar's Cottage. However, as Harriet continued to speak, she couldn't help but feel sucked in by Kareema nodding in assent, encouraging her to say more and more. And the more that Harriet spoke, the more the others at the table appeared to slip away, sliding gradually into the background, until it was only herself and Kareema who remained.

When — finally — Kareema held up her hand for Harriet to stop, just as she had done with Bella, Harriet felt like she had just undergone the most intensive therapy session of her entire life. Only when she breathed in, did she realise just how close to tears she was. She had spoken about her past career, about how wonderful it was to share her work with her friends, and how much happier she was. Perhaps it was the steeling look she received from George, but she managed to keep her emotions locked away.

"That's wonderful," Kareema said. "*Thank you*, Harriet."

Harriet felt a great sense of relief take hold as Kareema shifted her focus elsewhere; across the table, falling onto George, and then Robert, before finally going to Cassandra, since Bella had already had her say at the start.

When Kareema rose from the table, it was after noon. As Harriet rose with her, she studied Kareema's face, half wondering if she might find some sign of weariness there — bags under the eyes, a yawn coming on — but she detected nothing at all.

"There is nothing more to say, except to thank you for taking the time to explain yourselves to me personally. I hope to have a response by this evening." And, with that and nothing more, she trod out, leaving the assembled staff of Humble Greetings speechless.

About a minute after Kareema's footsteps had disappeared off into the distance of the castle, Robert and Bella began to speak among themselves, while Cassandra muttered a quiet excuse and slipped away, presumably back to her bedroom.

Harriet felt as if she had something warm and glowing in her chest. When she had first come here to meet with Kareema, she had never believed that she would end up feeling just as positive — just as *energised* — as she felt right at this moment.

Then she fixed her attention onto George.

And saw his grim expression.

Harriet's spirits immediately fell away.

And her smile slipped from her lips.

She frowned. "Did I do badly?" she whispered, so Bella and Robert wouldn't overhear.

George took hold of her forearm — a little roughly. "Come on," he said, his mouth close to her ear. "I'll explain."

George led her along several winding castle corridors with the expert ease of someone who hadn't just arrived the day before. As he whisked her on the way, Harriet had time to take in the various antechambers and doors on either side. To see into the cosy libraries, the numerous sitting rooms, and the guest bedrooms — all made up and awaiting visitors.

"In here," George said, somewhat gruffly, guiding her into one of the castle turrets.

The turret had been left unfurnished. There were gaps in the brickwork for archers to rain their arrows on invaders below. These gaps must've created a devilish draught.

George stood before her, his eyes on hers.

Harriet tried a smile, but George was unresponsive. She took a sharp breath, still feeling exhilarated about the conversation she had shared with Kareema. It was unlike anything else she had previously experienced — just how Kareema had managed to split her open and get her to say absolutely everything that was on her mind.

It was no wonder that Kareema was an expert in her trade.

"What do you think this is?" George asked her.

He kept his voice to a reasonable tone — to a flat, businesslike tone . . . but rather than offer her any form of reassurance, it only twisted her gut, put her on edge.

Harriet felt as if she had lead blocks weighing her feet down. "I was just . . . answering her questions . . . what was I supposed to . . ."

George drew a sharp intake of breath. "There was no need to go into all that detail, in front of us, in front of *Kareema* . . ."

Harriet thought about how — while George had been conversing with Kareema — she had prompted him for more details about his year to Australia, but George had remained sparse and vague, mentioning only the fruit-picking, and the 'wonderful cultural elements' he had discovered along the way. To her mind, George had come off worse — more wooden, stuffy — than she had in her chat with Kareema . . . because that was all it had seemed:

A *chat.*

Feeling a renewed sense of determination, Harriet turned on George. "She wanted us to be honest, and I'm sorry but I've never been a good liar. I thought it would be best just to tell the truth — I thought she might expect and appreciate that, I thought . . ."

Chin tucked into his chest, George was shaking his head. "Look," he said. "You've sat through enough meetings with me and Robert to know better — that business is *always* business." He looked her in the eye. "You can't show your hand that easily — you'll be eaten alive. You'll get *all* of us eaten alive."

Harriet allowed the thought to drift about her mind for no more than a matter of seconds. And then a rage such as she had never previously felt gripped her. When she turned on George, she saw his lips were parted, as if he was ready to dispense yet more advice.

But Harriet had different plans.

"I was just doing what came naturally. Do you understand how much of an *idiot* I've felt at Humble so far? Do you have *any* idea just how ridiculous I feel to be asking questions all the time, to never understand anything? To be . . ." she felt herself welling up now, but she was determined not to allow George the satisfaction ". . . to be *worthless*."

The two of them stood in silence — both apparently astounded by the remarks which Harriet had just jabbered out.

George stared back at her long and hard. Then his gaze hardened. "Sometimes I think the only reason Bella wants you involved at all is because you're friends."

Harriet had heard enough.

She stormed out.

21

THOROUGH WORKOUT

Sweat soaked George's forehead.

Every muscle in his body was tight — on the brink of screaming out in pain.

The air around him stank of sulphur.

It caught at the back of his throat, nearly choking him.

He gripped the handles of the cross-trainer more tightly still, staring out ahead, to the lochs and foothills set in twilight. His arms worked as pistons, yanking the poles back and forth, making a constant, well-oiled *zip-zip* sound.

On some other day, he might've appreciated this place for what it was: an unbelievable location for a gym . . . now, though — *right now* — he really wasn't in any kind of mood to appreciate anything. Quite frankly, he couldn't care less about the flocks of birds meandering over the landscape, carving gorgeous, swirling shadows over the world. He just wanted to be out of this place. He wanted to be away from *her* . . .

He pushed himself harder.

Pumped his arms harder.

Harder.

It felt good to work his body to destruction. It stopped him from thinking. It allowed him to break away from everything . . . from everything that had gone on that day, and everything that was *going* to go on later.

George ploughed forward. He took little notice of the display in front of him which showed the imaginary distance he had travelled; and he couldn't care less about the imaginary speed he was going, or the calories he had burned. He just wanted to escape.

To be *away*.

Losing control happened rapidly — too fast for him to comprehend.

One moment he was clenching the poles of the cross-trainer, suspended in mid-air, zipping along as fast as he could manage, and the next he was being catapulted forward.

He held his hands up to guard his face.

All the same, one of the cross-trainer poles caught his temple on the way past.

Pain seared through his brain.

Electricity fried his nerves.

Then he landed with a *thump* on the stone floor.

He lay on the ground, staring up at the ceiling. He was lying there, alone, for long enough to admit to himself that he was surprised not to be in utter agony following his fall. His heart throbbed in his throat. He thought for the longest time that he might choke — that his body might not be willing to throw him a lifeline. That this was the end. It would certainly have been a pathetic way for him to go. He thought of all the typical stories he had heard while he had been at Lord Charles's side, about all of those executives who — so anxious to prove themselves to be ever-young, virile, or whatever — would push themselves to the limit each day in the gym, despite their personal clinician's advice to the contrary, and more or less inevitably, be found in a sweaty, motionless heap hours later.

George had been determined never to be like that.

Never to allow himself to end up like that.

And yet, here he was right now, involved in what might well prove to be the most important business deal of his life . . . and he had just done exactly what he had promised himself he would never do . . . and all because of *some girl*.

He inhaled.

Felt an ache begin to take hold of his chest.

He wondered if he had broken a rib.

But then he realised there was some other reason.

Harriet wasn't just *some girl* . . . he knew that . . .

For better or worse, he had got himself into a 'situation', as they called it back in the city. Something he had been adamant to avoid.

He had always thought himself too clever — too *above it all* to get himself 'involved'.

And yet that was precisely what had happened.

As he lay still, on the stone blocks of Kareema Ashburton's Scottish castle, he started to feel the pain kicking in. Strangely, it began at the tips of his toes. And then it moved up his calves. Gripping his kneecaps for long seconds. Then it went all the way up his waist, and to his chest, where it settled — *quite happily* — all over his entire body.

He gritted his teeth, feeling himself throbbing all over.

Once he got over the initial burst of pain, he realised it was mostly sourced on his right side. As he took sharp, snorting breaths, the pain in other areas of his body dulled.

Nothing compared to the pain in his right side.

He tried to lever himself into a sitting position, but the pain was too much to bear. He soon returned to lying on the floor. The effort it had taken just to try and sit up had been like someone butting him in the stomach with a blunt object.

He allowed his eyelids to flutter shut, and he wondered if he was going to die in what was the most embarrassing manner he could conceive of . . . and all before he had had the chance to close the deal with Kareema Ashburton.

Life was very cruel indeed.

22

THE RETURN

*I*t had only been when Harriet had returned to her bedroom that she had recalled — with some disappointment — that George occupied the one beside her own.

That they shared a bathroom.

The first thing that she did — after securing her own bedroom door — was to make for the bathroom and to lock the door which led to George's bedroom. She allowed herself a sly grin as she turned the bathtub tabs, running hot water over the soap crystals provided.

She got out of her clothes and beneath the warm water. She began to lose herself in the heady scent of lavender, to feel the tingling sensation of the herbs up her nostrils and down her throat. She stretched out her limbs, quickly realising that the bathtub was by far the largest she had ever had the fortune of experiencing. It wasn't long before her thoughts left the present moment behind, beginning to wander.

In the darkness, she imagined herself swimming in some

distant tropical sea. She thought of turtles, and dolphins, and of countless tropical fish swimming about coral reefs.

Perhaps the answer was for her to leave Normonswold behind for a while.

She had always flirted with the idea of travelling the world — when would she get a better chance? She had some savings from her previous job . . . along with the money Bella had paid her for the 'work' she had done for Humble thus far . . . even as Harriet had thought she had escaped, she found herself returning to the present. To what George had said to her. It was only now — dwelling on his comments — that she realised just how excruciatingly painful it had been.

But was it only painful because there was a grain of truth?

Harriet tried to float away to the land of her imagination for another few moments, but she knew the effort was in vain. She knew there was no escaping. She opened her eyes.

The bathroom was dark. She had brought the doors shut behind her, not bothering to flip on the lights. She listened to her surroundings. She listened for the sounds of George next door. She had half expected to hear him arrive . . . she had thought he would attempt to open the bathroom door, to come through to her, and perhaps apologise.

If nothing else, she was certain he wanted to clear the decks before their meeting with Kareema Ashburton that evening. If there was any rumour about Kareema Ashburton which Harriet had no intention of doubting, it was her ability of perception. She was certain that Kareema would sense tension without even having to set foot in the same room.

Harriet sat up in the bath. She tucked her knees into her chest. She stared out into the darkness, still listening, waiting for George's giveaway footsteps . . . but, nothing . . .

Perhaps George had meant what he had said — maybe, instead of returning here to attempt some form of half-hearted, false apology, he had taken the most efficient business decision, and gone right to the root of the problem.

Had he gone to tell Bella what she had to hear?

That Harriet — friends though they may be — contributed nothing to Humble Greetings; that she was nothing better than dead weight. And that they would be much better off simply cutting her loose once and for all . . . 'it would be much kinder in the long run', and other clichés. Well, she was determined not to give them the satisfaction.

Decided she would be the one to make the first move, Harriet shifted out from the now lukewarm bathwater, grabbing her towel as she trudged towards the door leading back to her bedroom. Once inside, she looked to the ruby-red dress which had been left on the bed by the house staff while she had been in the bath. A cursory glance over the wardrobe revealed the clothes she had arrived to the castle in — blouse, trousers, and a cardigan.

She put her shoes on. Thank God she had worn flat-soled shoes, suitable for driving. She turned her back on the red dress lying across the bedsheets, feeling a slight buzz of romance. She thought of all the scenes in films she had witnessed through the years, and couldn't help but think that she was making a noble exit of a kind. As she trotted her way down the castle steps, her mind began to skip ahead, further convincing her that — albeit dramatic — this was the right course of action for her to be taking.

She simply had no other option than to cut and run.

To jump or be pushed.

It felt as if all her life she had been *pushed*.

And she wasn't going to be pushed any longer.

She reached the ground floor of the castle. She brushed past a succession of waiting staff who — although appearing surprised to see her there — only smiled and stood aside, allowing her to walk right out of the castle. She couldn't believe how easy it was for her to walk away. When she heard the gravel crunch beneath her shoes, she truly believed she had got away. And — what was more — she had made the right choice.

But then something stopped her.

An invisible hand . . . foresight.

Harriet turned around and looked at the castle behind her. She looked for any sign of pursuit — saw none at all. But then, why would anyone be pursuing her when they had all been given the run of the castle? When Kareema had trusted them in her own home?

Harriet could still turn back. She didn't have to leave all this behind. She could still face up to the meeting later that evening. She could still prove George wrong — prove to him she *was* important to Humble; that she did have something to offer after all.

And then there was the sense of creeping guilt.

She thought about how Bella would feel if she discovered Harriet had skipped out on them. That she had simply up and left before the big meeting with Kareema. Could Harriet really do that to her lifelong friend, after all they had been through together? And after they had kissed and made up after all these years . . .

She took a deep breath, trying to make the right decision, and trying to make it quickly. She knew there was little room for inde-cision — that there was no *time* for indecision. She needed to work out whether she was in or out. She thought about how there had been a time — not so long ago — when she had refused to believe she would ever be able to pass her driving test, but she had succeeded.

With George at her side, she had succeeded.

She thought about how patient George had been with her, and she thought of his reaction today. It was difficult to reconcile the two . . . but, then again, maybe she just had to admit to herself George wasn't perfect after all — perhaps she needed to let up, be patient with him.

Allow him that momentary loss of temper, or whatever the outburst — those hurtful things he'd told her — had represented.

Harriet trod back towards the castle, the same way she had left. The house staff remained as indifferent to her return as they had been to her departure. It surprised her to find she had somehow sketched the route back up to her bedroom in some part of her mind, that the castle no longer represented an unfathomable labyrinth.

She made her way back up the staircases to where she had come, and then snuck back into her room, almost on tiptoe, all too aware someone might overhear her re-entrance and confront her.

All too aware that George might overhear her.

But, when she got back into her bedroom, she heard nothing from the bathroom they shared, and neither did she hear anything from George's bedroom on the other side.

She looked to the ruby-red dress spread out before her on the bed, and then she decided it was time for her to get to work.

23

A HUMBLE MEETING

*H*arriet realised she was quaking all over — from head to toe — as she picked her way through the castle, following on the heels of a member of the house staff, heading for the meeting with Kareema Ashburton. Her environment was still overwhelming. The stone passageways, the ancient items which hung from the walls, and the occasional glances she got of the world through the narrow slits in the stonework.

Like the night before, the surrounding rolling hills and lochs were bathed in moonlight. The sky was clear. Stars twinkled down.

The member of the house staff left Harriet in a room replete with a candlelit long table, a blazing fireplace, and tapestries draping off the walls. Harriet felt a nudging disappointment to look at the faces already there, and see that George had yet to arrive. Or perhaps she was disappointed that she and George wouldn't have a moment alone together so that they might clear the air. She reminded herself just why she was there — just why they had gone to all the trouble of travelling up to Scotland . . . it was for the business, it was for Humble . . . and Harriet had made the decision that she was going to act professionally, although her reasons for doing so might be personal.

She looked to Bella and Robert, feeling a touch of anger flare in her to see how they pulled that traditional *couply* trick of speaking between themselves; blocking the rest of the world out by simply turning their backs and conversing in low tones. She turned her attention to Cassandra, who was browsing the tapestries, and sidled up beside her.

Harriet looked over the tapestry before them. It depicted what she could best describe as a hunting scene. There was a pack of dogs chasing a deer, with overexcited, long-bearded men on horseback galloping behind. "Inspiration for your next design?"

Cassandra gave her the glimmer of a smile. "Yes, actually. It's weird how inspiration comes to me. I pick it up from the weirdest places." Then she glanced over her shoulder, to Bella and Robert, before turning back to Harriet. "Did you hear about George?"

Harriet's heart thumped in her throat. She was ready for something — *anything*. And yet she found it impossible to form words. Thankfully, Cassandra continued without further prompting.

"He's been taken ill."

Harriet thought about how George had looked perfectly fine not more than an hour or so ago, albeit not in the best of moods. " 'Ill' ?"

Cassandra glanced again to Bella and Robert. "He's being tended to." Even despite herself, she couldn't help but give a slight smile. "Think he overdid it in the gym, from what I heard."

Harriet's panic calmed slightly, but didn't go away completely. She had at least lost the idea that he might be suffering from the sudden onset of some life-threatening fever. "Is he . . . not coming?"

Cassandra shook her head. "He needs to rest. That's what the doctor says."

"There's a doctor here?"

Even as the words passed between Harriet's lips, she knew the folly of them — of course Kareema Ashburton had a personal *doctor* . . . why wouldn't she?

It was then that — flanked by her assistant Sylvie — Kareema entered the room, and any chance for further conversation was brought to a halt.

The three representatives from Humble immediately fell into the kind of hush which might've been more ordinarily reserved for the arrival of royalty.

Kareema gestured for them all to take their places around the long table, and they obeyed. Harriet couldn't help noticing how Sylvie now took her place beside Kareema at the table, rather than waiting in one of the chairs arranged at the edge of the room. That calmed Harriet somewhat, to know Sylvie wasn't watching her on the sly. It was also a relief that they apparently seemed set for the meeting before they ate. It had been somewhat distracting — to say the least — when Harriet had been expected to concentrate on eating before speaking to Kareema . . . as kind as she had proven to be later.

"I see the castle has claimed a victim," Kareema said, with a broad smile.

Harriet felt a brief rush of fury at this remark. Perhaps it was not having seen George after his accident, or whatever it was that'd happened to him. Maybe if she had had the chance to see him before this meeting she would've felt calmer.

As it was, she was fuming — albeit with a pleasant smile on her lips.

"Never mind, I hope for this meeting to be brief." Kareema looked down the table, meeting each one of them by the eye. "I only wanted to tell you that I have decided to take your venture under further consideration — and that you are welcome to leave my home at a time of your choosing. I shall make you aware of my final decision in the next month. Is that acceptable to you?"

Harriet looked across the table, catching a glimpse at Robert's expression. Although he was clearly making an effort to hold his poker face — as he always was — Harriet was certain she noted a slight twitch at the corner of his eye. She knew that such a stickler for process and for plans would be rendered unnerved by Kareema's behaviour. She *had* told them that she would have a decision for them later on that evening — it was just not the final one which Robert had clearly assumed it would be.

Nobody said anything to Kareema's lingering question, and so she rose up out of her seat. Sylvie wasn't far behind. As the two of them made for the exit, Robert finally raised his voice. "And we can expect the reply in one month?" he asked, his voice much tighter, more wavering than usual.

Kareema met his eye, smiling broadly. "More or less." Then she slunk out of the room.

All of them sat in silence, none quite sure just what they had witnessed.

2 4

THE SICKBAY

*H*arriet had to stop and ask several times even after a member of the house staff had given her detailed instructions on how to locate the sickbay. She was certain she had gone up the three flights of steps, walked past two suits of armour, and then passed through an archway before climbing another flight of steps . . . and yet, she arrived to a cosy, vibrant-smelling greenhouse on the roof of the castle rather than any sort of medical facility.

As she took stock of the greenhouse, in moonlight from above, she saw it was a kitchen garden; that there was a whole assortment of herbs and spices for cooking. She breathed in the heady scents of basil, coriander, and mint. There was something homey about being up here. Something which reminded her of being back with Aunt Adiema.

After a few minutes' browsing, Harriet turned back, found a member of the house staff who took pity on her and led her to the sickbay where George was located.

As she passed through the doorway to the sickbay, she felt her stomach twisting. There was nothing much different about the décor of the sickbay when compared with the rest of the castle. For some reason, she had believed the place would be fitted out like a hospital ward; that the stone floors would be replaced by slick, vinyl matting, and that the walls would be white-washed, featureless. However, the only items which marked the sickbay as being different from the rest of the surrounding castle were the cabinets gathered around. Many of them had been left open, and Harriet could see various pieces of medical equipment within: gauze, disinfectant, a few syringes . . . all the essentials that might be required for a doctor serving their duty in the Backend of Beyond.

Like the rest of the castle at night, the sickbay was lit by electric-powered, imitation torches which hung from the walls. As with the rest of the castle, Harriet thought it lent the room an unnecessarily sinister air. She tried not to take too much notice.

George was lying on a bed across the room, alone. He was flat on his back, his arm extended over his forehead in a pose which reminded Harriet of an overwrought renaissance woman. He continued to stare out of the window as she approached, as if he didn't hear her footsteps.

Harriet looked to the chair beside the bed, and settled upon it.

She looked at the side of George's face, noting the large bruise at his temple. All of a sudden, she felt the weight upon her shoulders of their last meeting together, and she remembered the hurtful things he had told her. She felt anger, then despair, but she managed to keep both emotions bottled up. She had to be the patient one now.

Finally, George spoke, albeit with his gaze still fixed on the window outside. "Did you have the meeting with Kareema?"

Harriet held herself firm. She silently berated him for not bringing up their last parting — at least she was left in no doubt about just what George's priorities were . . .

"What did she say?"

"She hasn't got a response for us yet. She'll let us know in a month or so."

" 'A month or so' ?"

"Uh-huh."

George continued to look out the window for another few moments, then he turned to Harriet for the first time. She could better see the bruising at his temple now. Although she was far from being any sort of expert in injuries, it certainly looked like he had taken an almighty blow. "She didn't say anything else?" he asked. "Nothing about the meeting?"

Harriet shook her head.

George bowed his head slightly. Then he looked around the room. His shoulders rose and fell with a sigh and, although he tried to hide it, Harriet saw — without mistake — that he gave a wince of pain.

"Is it good news?"

George breathed in deeply, then stared at the ceiling. "I . . . don't really know."

Harriet felt a tightness form over her chest. She had become so used to George knowing absolutely everything about this alien world that it came as a shock to hear George admit he was as clueless as she was.

"I mean," George went on, "from what I've heard Kareema is direct — she doesn't play games. If she's not interested then she has no hesitation in bringing things to a close."

"So it is good news?"

George lingered a moment longer, staring into mid-air. When

he met Harriet's eye again, his stern expression lasted only a moment on his lips. Then — seemingly out of nowhere — a smirk appeared. "Well, it's better news than her flinging us from the castle turrets, I suppose."

Acting on impulse, Harriet reached for George's hand, lying on his stomach. Their skin brushed and she felt an electrical charge pass between the two of them. She half expected him to knock her hand away, to say something about their fling being a mistake. But he said nothing. And Harriet decided to take her chance, giving George's hand a squeeze.

Before Harriet could quite get her head around what was happening, George leaned into her. His hand flinched with pain. His lips pressed against her earlobe. "Shut the door."

Harriet wasted no time in shutting the door to the sickbay, bringing the wooden beam down to lock it. Her senses working too quickly to comprehend, she glanced about the room, apparently searching for other unsealed openings. There were none.

When Harriet returned to George's bedside, he had already cleared some space for her. She held back for a moment, unsure, and then decided this was the reason she had returned. She hadn't remained in the castle because of her childhood friend, but because she had been so afraid of ruining what she had with George.

What they had together.

She was tentative about touching his body. She didn't want to hurt him. And yet, at the same time, she had an almost uncontrollable lust ploughing through her. She so wanted to feel his bunched-up muscles beneath her fingertips, and she so wanted to feel the pump of blood beneath his skin, and she so *wanted* to feel their bodies locked together.

She slipped her dress over her head, depositing it on the floor. Then she returned to George's side. Every moment she spent away from him felt like a separate expanse of infinity, stretching on and on and on . . . and she was determined she wouldn't be denied any longer. That they wouldn't deny one another any longer.

She rose on top of George, breathing in his lingering musky scent. He was still in his gym clothes. There had been no time during his treatment for him to shower. And it only drove Harriet wilder. She arched her back over him, drawing his smell deeper into her body through her mouth and nostrils, feeling it fill her up entirely.

Until it felt as if she might burst.

As she sank back on her haunches, feeling George's powerful thighs beneath hers, she reminded herself to be gentle. That he was wounded.

But as she removed his shorts and explored his body, she felt his desire more than ever. His arms reached up around her, bringing her down on top of him. Before she knew it, she forgot even where they were . . . it was just the two of them.

Harriet rode on, feeling her whole body pulsing with a million invisible electric charges. There was a pulsing rhythm within her chest. She wanted nothing more than to scream out — to shake the whole castle with her pleasure.

But something held her back.

Some sense of decorum.

Some sense of *respect* for Kareema Ashburton.

As she felt herself rocking harder and harder, George's body locked up several times. She knew she had to be causing him pain, and yet he urged her onwards, constantly squeezing her hands, his husky voice demanding that she not stop.

So she didn't stop.

When she felt herself nearing a climax, the room became very small. She felt as if it was drawing in tightly upon itself. The sensation wasn't uncomfortable or distressing — on the contrary, there was something reassuring about the space surrounding her and George becoming more compressed. Because it served to bring them closer together.

To make them more united.

As Harriet began to feel her strength deserting her, as she felt incapable of making the final effort to bring the two of them to the end, George pulled her down on top of him once more. She felt his hard chest up against her breasts, and felt his warm breath down the side of her neck. "I'm so sorry," he whispered.

Her whole body froze for a moment. And then — realising precisely what he had said — her tension loosened. "I'm sorry too," she whispered back in his ear.

She clung onto him for the longest time, feeling their heartbeats mingle, and meet, and then drift apart again. She felt his whole body hard beneath her own. His body was damp with sweat, and — *she realised* — effort at the pain he was feeling.

Harriet was on the brink of withdrawing, of giving George some much needed space so that he could undergo his prescribed rest and relaxation, but he drew her back down to him, even tighter this time. With his lips close to her ear, she could barely make out his voice — she supposed she had worn him out more than she could imagine.

"I love you," he said.

Harriet felt her whole body shudder, as if someone had run an ice cube down her spine. She composed herself, and then leaned into his ear. "I love you too."

RECOVERY

*G*eorge felt light flooding the room. He looked about him, expecting to see Harriet lying by his side, gently sleeping. He was shocked to find he was alone. He looked across the room, to the cabinets filled with medical supplies. He wondered what time it was, and decided — from the strength of the light — that it had to be mid-morning.

It was then that he heard the sound of bare feet against stone.

He turned to the door, expecting to see his doctor step through.

It wasn't his doctor, however.

Wearing the same ruby-red dress she had been wearing the previous night, when she had paid him a visit, Harriet stepped through the doorway. She was bearing a covered silver tray, and a smirk that would have made him proud. As she approached, her smirk widened into a full smile. She set the tray down on his bedside table then took a seat on the edge of his mattress. "You wouldn't believe how much of a fight the member of the house staff put up with me. The girl *really was* quite set on serving you breakfast in bed."

Even though George felt pain tingling at the tips of seemingly every nerve in his body, he reached out and ran his hand up Harriet's spine. "How did you ever convince her?"

"Who said anything about 'convincing' her? I just pushed her right off one of the battlements."

They laughed.

George reached for the tray, only to feel a flash of heat in his chest. He withdrew, doing his best to hide his reaction from Harriet. But he knew there would be no fooling her.

Harriet looked on at him with concern. "Should I go and fetch the doctor?"

George squeezed his eyes closed, hoping blackness would help him concentrate on pushing the pain away. "No," he replied. "It's fine." He opened his eyes again, allowing the bright light of the sickbay back into his mind. He allowed himself a moment to get used to it, then turned his attention back onto Harriet. "What's the plan for today?"

" 'The plan' ?" Harriet replied. "Yes, the plan. You're doing a very good job of rubbishing any plans we're attempting to cobble together, as a matter of fact. I just had breakfast with the others, oh . . ." she looked up, over his head, and he realised there was a clock there ". . . some three, four hours ago. It'll be lunch soon. We *were* planning to leave after we'd all had something to eat, and the doctor had had another chance to look you over." She cocked her head to one side. "Although judging from last night, there seems to be very little wrong with you."

George felt himself flush slightly. He smiled back. "What the doctor doesn't know won't hurt her." Feeling a stirring in his stomach, he turned to the breakfast tray.

"Please," Harriet said, removing the silver lid on the tray. "Allow me."

Breakfast turned out to be a bowl of fruit, cereal, orange juice, coffee — cold now — and a rack of wholemeal, buttered toast — also cold.

Even despite the pain which panged him with seemingly every bite, George managed to get the breakfast down. He supposed he had built up quite a hunger in the past few hours. All this 'rest and recovery' was an exhausting business.

"So," he said, finally finished with his breakfast, "what's the modified plan?"

"To leave as soon as you're ready." Harriet glanced over her shoulder, as if she expected Kareema Ashburton herself to be standing there, casting a watchful glare over them. She turned back to him. "The last thing we want is to outstay our welcome — albeit I have to admit that the décor here is going to be difficult to leave behind. I don't suppose you have room in your car to haul that bathtub back to Normonswold?"

"I don't think it would do the suspension any good."

Harriet organised his breakfast tray, and then took it away. He watched as she left his room and he felt nothing but a wrenching sadness deep within his chest to think that — after all those painful things he had said to her the previous night — she had had every right to walk out; to never see him again.

But she had come back.

And she had told him that she loved him.

Just as he had told her . . .

About ten minutes later, Sylvie appeared in the doorway.

"Oh, sorry," Harriet said. "Does the doctor need to see George?"

Sylvie smirked. "Yes, she does."

Harriet rose up from where she had been perching on the edge of the mattress. "I'll give the doctor some room."

"Really, it's fine," Sylvie replied. "You can stay — we're fairly informal about protocol here."

Harriet was clearly unsure how to react. Then, with a glance at George, and a nod, she took the cue to go and sit down in the chair over by the window.

George realised he hadn't taken the time to explain that Sylvie was also his doctor . . .

Sylvie rolled up her blouse sleeves and set her attention onto George. "How've you been getting on? Any change in the level of pain, or about the same?"

George reclined against the headboard, preparing for his examination. "About the same."

"Okay."

George was receptive to the various pokes and prods about his body, and the relentless questioning of 'On-a-scale-of-one-to-ten-how-much-does-*this*-hurt?'.

Sylvie soon discharged him, giving him some pain medication to be getting on with, while being tentatively diagnosed with bruised ribs and a slight concussion. If only he could use the 'slight concussion' he had sustained in the gym last night to explain the way he had acted towards Harriet.

He had had the best interests of Humble at heart, and yet he had been so wrong to go about it in the way he had.

As he left the sickbay behind, Harriet gave him a playful punch on the arm.

And a wry smile.

"Why didn't you tell me that Sylvie was no ordinary PA?"

"I thought that much was obvious."

THE LONG ROAD HOME

*I*t was only when they were back down in the garage, where they had left their cars, that Harriet realised that — given George's injuries — there would be no choice but for her to drive them all the way home. As she got in behind the wheel, she couldn't help but wonder how many newly qualified drivers had had the experience of being flown through the air by a helicopter. It almost made her feel as if she was ready for anything.

She helped George to collapse the passenger seat into a reclined position, and then — despite his protests — eased him into the car. As she did so she felt him flinch in pain even despite the painkillers the doctor had given him. Once he was ready, she got into the driver's seat, took a deep breath, and then readied herself for the journey ahead.

Why Harriet had thought that it would be any different this time — that they *wouldn't* have taken the helicopter back the way they had come — she had no idea.

No sooner had she driven them out of the garage, and a little way out into the open, than did she hear the familiar chopping of the helicopter rotor blades above. She didn't turn her attention from the road as she felt the car being lifted into the air.

They were set back down with a bump on the exact same road the helicopter had lifted them off from. She supposed that Kareema Ashburton's administration was more than a little accustomed to providing visitors this sort of service.

Even though Harriet had a slight panic after an hour of driving, to think that George could do nothing much to help her from where he was lying on the passenger seat, she managed to get them back to Normonswold with no fuss.

She felt a sense of deep satisfaction — such as she had never previously felt — when she drove them on past the village boundaries. There was a moment when she realised she was unsure about just where to take George, and then — suddenly decided — she pulled up outside her Aunt Adiema's home. There was no way she was going to drop him off at the Thicket Arms Inn to fend for himself. Albeit, that was just what George appeared to have in mind considering his protests as she helped him from the back seat, and over the threshold where — having been warned earlier — Aunt Adiema was faithfully waiting in the kitchen, with a cup of tea, a blanket, and a hot water bottle.

Again, against the backdrop of his protests, Harriet eased George down into a chair in the sitting room. Although he upheld his flawless manners throughout, Harriet couldn't help but notice the slight wince which crossed his lips as Aunt Adiema plumped his pillows and inadvertently knocked his shoulder.

Once George was tucked into the armchair with a thick blanket, Maximilian appeared out of precisely nowhere and leaped up to settle himself in George's lap.

Harriet had no time to ask whether or not George was a cat person.

For no more than five minutes, Harriet slipped into the kitchen to make George a sandwich, but when she returned to the sitting room, George and Maximilian were already fast asleep. With a glance to Aunt Adiema, Harriet decided to let him rest — he *had* had more of a workout than her aunt might have imagined . . .

Although Harriet had thought that she would be exhausted following the drive down from Scotland, when she tried to lie down in bed to get some rest, no sense of sleepiness overtook her. She just lay there staring at the ceiling, thinking about Kareema Ashburton's castle, and wondered just what would happen next.

If the trip had been worthwhile.

Not finding any rest at home, she decided to take a walk out into the falling Normonswold twilight. It was still early, not having yet gone seven o'clock.

Aunt Adiema accompanied her.

It didn't seem that Harriet had much choice in the matter.

On their way through the village, they bumped into Dorothy.

He was dressed in a suit, apparently not yet having changed out of his work wear. He waited outside the Thamses' cottage. It was only after they had greeted one another that — with a toe-curling *screech* — Harriet realised Dorothy was not alone.

Indigo Miles tottered down the garden path, pausing only to bring the gate shut behind her with a *clatter*.

"Dear!" she said, turning to Harriet. "I had no *idea* you were planning on *returning* so soon!"

Harriet felt beleaguered for a few moments. She glanced to

Dorothy and Aunt Adiema, as if they might be able to help her answer the question. She turned back to Indigo. "We, uh, just got back . . . about an hour ago."

Indigo lurched forward, grabbing Harriet by the forearm and giving her a — quite painful — squeeze. "Then *how* was it? What did you *do*? Did everything *come off* as you'd hoped?"

To be quite honest, although Harriet had a basic idea of what they had gone to Kareema Ashburton to achieve, she couldn't help but feel as if she was something of an imposter — the wrong person to ask about such things. But she responded all the same. "Fine, I think," she replied.

Indigo's smile widened. She patted Harriet's arm with an almost elemental force. "Good, good!" She looked about, and then gave a dramatic sigh. "Old Couples' Café, then?"

Harriet had to admit she had been looking forward to an evening walk after such a long drive, but at the same time she knew not many people turned down an invitation from Indigo Miles and lived to tell the tale.

Thankfully, Geoffrey and Diana — the proprietors of Old Couples' Café — had arranged chairs in the street outside so she would be permitted some fresh air at the very least. Once they had all sat down, Harriet amused Indigo Miles greatly by deciding to order a glass of freshly squeezed lemonade rather than the standard cup of tea. She was half hoping Indigo Miles might throw her out of the meeting for having the nerve, but if she did find it a 'lack of spirit', or some other nonsense, then she hid it behind a blinding grin.

It surprised Harriet to see the red-haired girl from the party —

Jeanie — emerge from the café bearing the teas and the lemonade. Then again, Harriet supposed working at Old Couples' Café was something of a rite of passage for anyone growing up in Normonswold.

As Jeanie set the lemonade down in front of Harriet, they exchanged a smile.

Somehow, Indigo Miles had conspired to occupy the seat beside Harriet, and she was using the advantage to give her sharp nudges in the ribs with her elbow whenever she got the chance. These sharp nudges were unfailingly accompanied by a knowing wink . . . just exactly what she was winking about, Harriet didn't know.

Thankfully, she hadn't long to wonder.

Indigo Miles had no intention of allowing Harriet to sit there and sip at her lemonade.

After a polite pause passed over the table, Indigo turned her full force onto Harriet. "So," she began, "I've heard that congratulations are in order."

The first thing Harriet thought about was the meeting with Kareema Ashburton.

But Indigo had already grilled her on that.

Harriet looked about the others' faces, hoping one of them might be able to throw her a rope . . . but everyone was suddenly staring in completely opposite directions, apparently utterly uninterested in what Indigo Miles was asking.

"George?" Indigo said, inclining an eyebrow.

"Oh," Harriet replied, beginning to blush now. "Yes . . . *George*."

"Where is he?"

"Uh, he's sustained a . . . an injury."

Indigo Miles's voice soared high and blunt. "*Really?*"

"He was in the gym, and . . ."

Already Harriet felt as if she was betraying George's confidence. She really didn't want to have to speak for him. In actual fact, she hadn't got the full details about George's accident herself. She was the wrong person to ask.

"So you drove all the way back from Scotland?"

Harriet nodded.

Indigo clapped her hands together and cackled.

A pigeon — a little way off along the alleyway — was startled and took to the air.

"Wonderful, wonderful!" Indigo said, to nobody in particular.

Harriet couldn't help but wonder if Bella might be nearby. She seemed to be just about the only person in the vicinity with any sort of ability to contain her mother . . . then again, it wasn't like she was being *overly* intrusive; she was just being loud . . .

"And when can we expect the sound of wedding bells?" Indigo lurched forwards and slapped Harriet on the thigh. "Just joking, just joking!"

Harriet drew in her stomach and eyed her lemonade, trying to work out what the most painless way of extracting herself from this situation would be. Perhaps she could knock over her glass, pour lemonade all over herself and go home on the pretext of 'getting changed' . . . and of course George was at home, too, and she could check on him, and . . .

It was then that Harriet heard the familiar bell above the door to Old Couple's Café.

She glanced over and saw Jeanie emerge.

"Can I get you anything else?" she asked.

"More tea, I think, Jeanie dear!" Indigo replied.

Jeanie nodded, pressing her lips tightly together as she returned to the café.

Harriet saw her opportunity. She glanced to Indigo. "Excuse

me just a moment," she said, getting up from the table before Indigo had the chance to respond.

Harriet just about managed to squeeze herself in through the gap in the closing door, staying on Jeanie's heels. She caught Jeanie before she managed to get behind the counter and head into the kitchens where no doubt Geoffrey and Diana — *or both* — would be waiting with another job for her to do.

"Hi."

"Hi," Jeanie replied, looking flushed, slightly taken aback.

Realising she didn't have much in the way of a plan — beyond getting away from the conversation outside — she got out the first thing that occurred to her. "How's Daniel?"

"Daniel?" For the first time, Jeanie smiled. "Oh, he's fine. Things are fine. I spoke to him, like you told me."

"And what did he say?"

Jeanie averted her gaze. "Well, to tell the truth, he wasn't happy at all — but at least I had known to predict it. Kind of how I thought he would react . . . he surprised me, though."

"What'd he do next?"

Jeanie smiled. "He said we can look for somewhere to live here, then look for somewhere to rent in the city, you know, so that we can work there . . ." She flipped a glance around the café. "Make no mistake, I'm grateful to Geoffrey and Diana, but I don't see myself here in ten years' time. Not unless things go horribly wrong . . ."

"Sounds perfect."

Jeanie shrugged slightly. "Yeah, I feel happier about it." Then she openly grinned before lurching forwards.

Harriet had no time to react. When Jeanie collapsed into her, she barely managed to remain standing. Harriet was glad to be so close to the wall so she didn't fall over.

"Thank you *so* much," Jeanie said, her voice muffled against

Harriet's neck. "I'm so glad you told me what you did — otherwise things might've gone on like that for . . . well, maybe not too much longer." She pulled herself away from Harriet slightly, her eyes now a little damp. "I really love him," she said. "And I have no idea what I would've done without him — where I would've *gone* without him."

Although Harriet wasn't convinced she had had even the smallest of effects on Jeanie, she was more than happy to take her word for it.

"Hey," Jeanie said, looking over her shoulder, apparently catching sight of Diana peeping out from the kitchen doorway, "I need to get back to work." She reached down and squeezed Harriet's hand. "We'll talk later, okay?"

And, with that, Jeanie took off for the kitchens, but she didn't make it through the doorway before Harriet had had the chance to get the last word in.

"Any chance I could sneak out the back door?"

Jeanie froze a moment then broke into a fresh grin. "This way," she said, waving her on.

27

STEPPING UP

$\mathcal{H}$arriet passed her days just as she had done before the visit to Kareema Ashburton's castle in Scotland. She went to work, and she shadowed Robert as he went about his daily duties, visiting various distributors. She came to learn about how Humble was growing one day at a time — one contact at a time. They were slowly gaining a foothold in the world, becoming more secure with each step. And Harriet began to see where she might fit in.

Whereas she hadn't had any idea where she might fit into Humble when she had first started, now she saw how things had grown, how Bella had *foreseen* the business growing. She saw there would be far too much work for Robert and George alone to handle, and from a slightly removed position, she observed how Robert's main duties were devoted to the day-to-day running of the business, masterminding the finances and organisation rather than pressing hands — pressing on even more smiles — in office after office.

That was precisely where Harriet and George would be able to help out.

Although Harriet wasn't completely sure it was a single day which changed her mind — which made her *believe* she could yet fit in at Humble — it was shortly after their return from Kareema's castle that she felt the change taking place.

It took George a good few weeks before he was able to come to work as usual, and even then he required the aid of a crutch, although Harriet often found it discarded against a wall in a misguided attempt to go it alone.

Whenever she studied George's face after he had ditched the crutch, a slight wince took hold of the corner of his mouth with each step he took. She was careful not to openly scold him, though, instead allowing him to manage his condition on his own — he had all the pills, and all the medical advice, that he could wish for.

It was up to him whether or not he was going to obey.

It was a month or so after their visit to Kareema's castle when George declared himself fit enough to attend business meetings again. She couldn't help but notice the look of delight on Robert's face when George informed him that he could take up the day's business meetings. Harriet well knew that Robert was greatly looking forward to tackling the mountain of paper piling up in the office; that he wanted nothing more than to bring some order to the madness he believed was taking place all around him.

She had a routine now.

Every day, she would dig through the wardrobe at Molinaar's Cottage to find something suitably professional. Once she had given herself a good going over in front of the makeup mirror, she headed out the door.

Although today was the first day in a while that George was back on the job — that she wasn't accompanying Robert to meetings — he looked flawless as always. She made a point of staying clear of him as he hobbled his way down the garden path to the waiting car, reluctantly resting his weight on his crutch as he went.

Harriet was already halfway around the car to the passenger side when George spoke up. "I don't think I can manage driving just yet."

Harriet looked him in the eye, smiled.

George smiled back. "It's okay," he replied. "If you managed to get us all the way down from Scotland in one piece then I think you'll be all right getting us into the city and back."

Again, Harriet made a point of holding back from George, watching as he struggled to open the back passenger door to lay his crutch down across the seat. Then — when he caught her looking — she busied herself with getting into the driver's side of the car.

They didn't say much as they left Normonswold behind.

Harriet, though, did glance up in the rear-view mirror to the field which had once been bought by George's former employer — Lord Charles — so that it might serve as the Knightly Resort and Leisure Complex. The whole field had gone fallow now. She wondered whether Lord Charles had cut his losses and sold the land off . . . she supposed it didn't matter any longer; not now Lord Charles had given up Normonswold for a bad job.

Once they made it out onto the motorway, Harriet felt her mind begin to stretch out and away from her. It was funny to think she used to concentrate so hard whenever she was behind the wheel — that nothing about controlling the car had come naturally to her. Now, though she was afraid to say it out loud, driving on the motorway had an almost hypnotic effect on her. In a funny way, it was almost like a waking dream.

"So, how do you feel about taking the lead today?"

Harriet held her eyes on the traffic out ahead. She blinked a couple of times, bringing her mind clear. The closer they got to the city, the more congested it became. " 'The lead' ?"

"Yeah, you know? You can be the one who does all the talking — you should know how it goes well enough now, shouldn't you?"

Harriet thought for a moment, trying to work out whether or not she did. She was wary of George's confidence tricks. She was almost entirely convinced that George had magical mind-control powers. There was something about him which made her feel taller, which made her feel more confident. As if she could do anything.

And it seemed only natural for her to agree.

The reality of what George was proposing — that she take the 'lead' — only seeped into her mind when she caught sight of the monolithic building up ahead.

She glanced to George, wondering if he was going to have second thoughts, if he was going to give her a smile, then a condescending pat on the back of her hand, telling her that he had better 'take control' of the encounter after all. But he said nothing. He only sat still in the passenger seat as she pulled into the parking bay designated for visitors.

The offices belonged to a nationwide chain of garden centres, known as Green Thumbs. The logo over the entrance depicted an enormous thumb — aptly, though a little strangely, turned green — while the reception desk was covered in ivy.

Within the offices, everyone wore green polo shirts with the same Green Thumbs logo embroidered onto the breast pocket. Harriet couldn't help but feel as if she was a touch overdressed to be wearing a trouser suit, but at least George was dressed in a suit too.

The meeting room itself was in a courtyard, with a complete deckchair-and-table set laid out. Harriet supposed it was meant to possess a slightly kitsch quality — to show them that the spirit of the garden centres pervaded even the administration sector of the business. Harriet took a seat on one of the sun loungers, not quite feeling comfortable enough to bring her feet up onto the leg rest. George, however, didn't have as many reservations, no doubt seeing an opportunity to take the weight off his aching body. He reclined in his sun lounger, looking up to the overcast sky above the courtyard.

Harriet toyed with her briefcase catches, unsure quite what she should prepare by means of a visual aid. If George had told her with more anticipation, then she certainly would've spent the previous night going over everything at her disposal, working out the way she might prepare the perfect pitch. That, though, she supposed, had been George's aim. He had wanted to see how well she could perform on all that she had absorbed so far.

Harriet had got as far as mentally preparing the first sentence of the opening speech she would deliver to the buyers at Green Thumbs, when the three of them entered the courtyard.

Harriet's heart thumped against her ribs. She felt her throat constrict. But she took a deep breath. She knew she was just suffering from nerves. Nothing abnormal about that. She had to *expect* to be nervous. That was what would give her talk an edge — that was what would keep her on her toes and in the mood to sell what Humble had to offer. She could still recall *that* pep talk which George had given her about nerves.

When she glanced over at George, slowly working his way up from the sun lounger, she felt a pang of anger that he had thrust her into this situation with such little chance to prepare. But he would jump in and save her if she began to make an absolute fool of herself . . . wouldn't he?

The chief buyer — wearing a polo shirt, like everyone else at Green Thumbs — smiled brightly at Harriet. "Ursula," she said. "Pleased to meet you."

"Harriet."

Ursula glanced over her shoulder to the man and woman on her heels. "And this is Lisa and Terry."

Harriet exchanged glances with Lisa and Terry, before realising she was right in the middle of an awkward pause. She looked to George, seeing him standing at her shoulder, a firm, pleasant smile on his lips. But he remained silent, saying nothing. Then Harriet recalled *she* was supposed to be in control here.

"Uh, this is George, my . . . associate . . ."

George shook hands with Ursula, Lisa and Terry, and then Ursula ushered them down onto the garden furniture which served as the meeting room. Harriet had to admit she was glad it was a warm, sunny day. She wondered if they held their meetings in this courtyard rain or shine . . . that — she supposed — would show Green Thumbs' dedication to gardens, and the Great Outdoors, if nothing else.

Harriet breathed in deeply.

Prepared herself.

Looked Ursula directly in the eye.

And then did her best.

The meeting passed in a blur.

Harriet tried to get to grips with just what was playing out as it played out — but in the end there was simply no time. She just reacted to the situation, drawing on what had seemed to be insufficient past experience. Now, though, it all came naturally. She stopped getting in her own way and allowed it to come out. When she felt herself slipping into the higher gears, asking these executives for the sale — for them to stock Humble Greetings cards — she thought she might be about to blush.

But she managed to hold herself together.

To keep a cool head.

And to do what George and Robert made look so effortless every day of their working lives.

Before she knew quite what she had done, she was shaking hands with the grinning representatives of Green Thumbs, and being bid a glad farewell as she and George retreated through the offices, returning to the car waiting outside.

It was only when Harriet sat behind the wheel that she began to feel heat rising in her cheeks —the urge to cry became almost overwhelming. That was when she felt George's touch. His hand on her thigh. There was something about his fingers, about how they could send out warming waves through their tips. As if he could will her into a receptive, relaxed state. She wondered how different her life might've been if only she had met him a decade earlier. Would she have wasted so much time?

"Back to base?" Harriet asked, turning the ignition, preparing to back out.

"Back to base."

Just as she had done that morning, she found driving effortless. She glided the car through the mid-morning traffic. If someone had asked her to describe the panic she had once felt at getting behind the wheel, then she would've been unable. It was as if she had left everything about her former self behind.

In only a matter of months she had become unrecognisable.

And it instilled in her the sense that she could do anything.

Anything at all.

It was with this thought in mind that she eyed the signpost at the side of the motorway which read: BIRD RESERVATION.

Without so much as the twitch of an eyelid, she pulled off the road.

"Uh, this isn't the exit," George put in, from the passenger seat.

Harriet said nothing.

George straightened up, wincing slightly. He rubbed at his ribs, offering Harriet a rare glimpse of his vulnerability. "It's okay," George said, "you can just come around the bend here, re-join over the roundabout, then it's just —"

Harriet dropped a gear and revved the engine, drowning out his words.

She could feel George staring at the side of her face. She wondered if he believed she had gone insane — if he would try and grab the steering wheel off her. She was certain that she could fend him off if he tried . . . he was wounded, after all.

She followed the sign for the bird reservation, leading up a long slope. There were rolling hills either side now, and she soon lost sight of the motorway in her rear-view mirror. The sun glimmered at the edge of her vision and it seemed to set a fiery heat in the pit of her stomach. It made her feel powerful.

Unstoppable.

With a jerk of the wheel, she brought the car around the bend.

Out of the corner of her eye, she saw George reach up with his good arm for the handle above the passenger side window. He was clinging on, truly terrified now.

She wondered how he felt to be the one in the dark.

To not know what was going on.

Harriet pulled the car into the car park designated as part of the bird reservation. It being a weekday, the car park was deserted. She instinctively made for the large oak tree at one end of the car park, and — more importantly — the ample cover provided by its overhanging branches thick with leaves. This was perfect. Even better than she could've imagined. She drove through the dangling foliage, bringing the car underneath.

She pulled on the handbrake, shut off the engine.

Now they were hidden.

Nobody knew where they were.

That they were even here.

Harriet undid her seatbelt. She clambered over the handbrake, so that she sat in George's lap — so that she bore down on him.

In control.

She heard his snatched inhalations, and felt his warm breath against her neck. She could smell the delicious scent of honey which was clinging to him today. And she reached up to pin his muscular shoulders against the passenger seat. His eyes pierced her own.

There was terror, panic . . . *excitement.*

She wasted no more time.

She took hold of his tie, yanking it loose from around his throat.

She undid his shirt buttons.

Exposed his chest.

Pressed her hands there, feeling his heart beating.

His pulse was broad, and thick, and *powerful.*

She brought her mouth onto his.

Pressed her tongue in through his lips.

Breathed him in completely.

She could feel his hands working to free her from her blouse —

pulling her hair from the tight bun she had pinned it into earlier this morning.

There was nothing and nobody else now.

Only the two of them.

The world they had once known had been left behind forever.

She loosened his trousers, shrugging them into the floor space, allowing them to be forgotten for the time being. Then she embraced him more tightly than ever. She could feel him trembling and she wondered if she was hurting him. With a wicked thrill, she realised she just didn't care . . . not for the moment.

Pain was only temporary, after all.

Just like pleasure.

She reached down the side of the chair, feeling for the lever . . . she gave it a hard tug and the seat sprung backwards into a reclined position.

Feeling in total command now, Harriet rose on top of George, squeezing him between her thighs. She stared deep into his eyes and then pressed herself hard against him.

As she rode him to climax, she felt as if the tight space of the car — sheltered beneath the oak tree — was their own personal refuge.

Nobody would ever find them here.

28

BUSINESS AS USUAL

*G*eorge looked himself over in the long mirror at the room he rented at the Thicket Arms Inn. He had just got out of the shower and was wearing only a towel. He had needed a good wash after he had got back from the business meeting with Harriet . . . it still stretched his mind into all sorts of uncomfortable shapes to think about what'd happened; about how she had . . . well, there was no other way to put it . . . she had *jumped* him. But the extreme love-making session hadn't been without its consequences, as he was discovering now.

He eyed his side in the mirror and gently brought his arm upwards, feeling the muscle pulling tight as he did so. As he raised his arm higher and higher, he managed to convince himself that he would be able to go all the way this time . . . that he would —

With a pang of pain, he had no choice but to allow his arm to go slack.

To hang back down at his side.

His heart was pounding and he could feel his pulse pattering away at his temples.

How could he have been so *stupid?*

He had gone over the episode in his mind multiple times, wondering about the state of mind which'd led him to push so hard in the gym.

What had he been trying to prove?

Had Harriet really affected him so profoundly that he had had no recourse but to relieve his repressed aggression in the form of a high-intensity gym workout?

George breathed in deeply, regaining his composure as best he could. Then he tried to bring his arms up both at the same time. He felt the same tensing of the muscles, and then the same warning hint of pain . . . before he could reach the top of his range, the pain became almost too much to bear.

Almost.

Because this time he held on.

He sank his teeth into his lower lip, tasting blood.

He was determined.

When he breathed in, his whole body shuddered. It felt as if the pain was aching right down to his bones. As if someone had injected molten lava into his veins.

He held on for a few moments longer.

Until he couldn't anymore.

His arms dropped again.

And his whole body was racked with pain.

He doubled over, panting, squeezing his eyes shut, making tight fists.

It wasn't fair . . . how one moment of madness could lead to weeks and weeks of pain.

When he managed to get some sort of a hold back on himself, he began to pace his room at the inn. He thought about Harriet.

About what they had just done.

About how he had told her that he *loved* her.

And then he thought about the argument which they'd had . . . the one which'd led to his injury. He thought about how his whole life had been built upon control — albeit not to the extent that Robert had built his life upon control — but he had always prided himself on being the one to pull the strings. And it hurt him to think that someone else had something over him. That someone else had *power* over him.

And yet, hadn't there been a part of himself which'd enjoyed losing control?

Which'd *savoured* the feeling of being helpless to another's will?

George untucked himself from his current position, and — heart still beating wildly — he took a seat on the edge of the bed. He stared at the patterned wallpaper, hoping its design might be some sort of cryptic puzzle for him to solve. But all he could see were swirls and geometric lines.

God, how had he become so *lost*?

And what was he doing in this place, in the back end of beyond . . . in Normonswold?

To think that when he had first visited the place with Lord Charles he had believed it would be nothing more than a few weeks' stay while Lord Charles fulfilled his latest flight of fancy. That made him smirk.

What a mess.

He turned to look out of the window, to the village streets, bathed in the evening sunset. The year in Australia should have cleared his mind. He had thought that when he returned to the UK, he would see the path ahead . . . and yet all those offers had come in and not one of them had swayed him . . . not until Bella Miles had got in touch.

And now he had got in over his head.

Kareema Ashburton.

And everything *she* entailed.

It was only in the past few days — expecting a response to come at any moment — that he had allowed himself to accept the idea that she might reject the deal.

That she might reject Humble.

That she might reject *him*.

For someone who had never been rejected for anything — or by anybody — in his entire life, he was certain it would be a gigantic shock. And one which he had managed to convince himself he would never be able to get over.

It would break him.

If Kareema said no he was . . . done.

Just thinking about the word — *no* — took his breath away.

Like a punch to the gut.

He breathed in again, feeling as if his thoughts were bouncing off the confines of his skull. He rolled his shoulders, the pain still lingering, still causing his nerves to twitch.

He had to get out.

He had to *get away*.

Before it was too late.

29

RUNAWAY

The day following her meeting with George at Green Thumbs, Harriet felt an extra skip in her step. Like the day before, the sun was shining, but there was a pleasant breeze blowing too. There was little doubt that this would turn out to be the most beautiful day of the year so far. At breakfast, Aunt Adiema asked her what she was so happy about, and when Harriet told her the news about the deal she had done the previous night — she had returned late from Humble having opened a celebratory bottle of wine with Bella, Robert and Cassandra — Aunt Adiema was quietly impressed. With folded arms, and a slight smile twisted onto her lips, she congratulated Harriet, before hastening to add that she could still have a very successful career of another kind if she so chose to run the riding school.

Harriet made gracious noises and slunk out of the house.

Her good mood remained with her all the way up the garden path of Molinaar's Cottage, right until she turned the doorknob and stepped over the threshold.

She felt the tension straightaway.

Whereas the house was usually somewhat manic — with Robert's dog Woss, running wild, wagging his tail at everyone and everything; and with some kind of music turned up loud in the kitchen while a kettle boiled away on the stove — today the ambience was completely devoid of anything. Not a sound, it seemed.

To start with, Harriet thought that everyone might be in the garden, that the simple explanation was that there was nobody in the house.

But once she had gone through the front hall and entered the kitchen, she saw all of Humble's staff — minus George — present at the table.

Not one of them even had a cup of tea.

There was an unopened envelope sitting on the table between them.

Harriet's smile slipped from her lips. She looked everyone in the eye, each person in turn looking pallid, despite the warm weather outside. She saw that Woss was sitting upright in the corner of the room, still, his head cocked to one side, watching the table with everybody else. "Who's the letter from?" Harriet asked.

"Kareema," Bella replied, turning her attention onto the letter.

"Why haven't you opened it yet?"

Robert spoke up. "We wanted to wait for everybody to get here. We didn't want anybody to be the last to know."

"So we're just waiting for George?"

Another short silence, and then Cassandra spoke up. "Harriet, George is gone."

Harriet heard the words pass Cassandra's lips, but her brain somehow failed to process them. " 'Gone' ? How do you mean?"

Robert replied, "We've been trying to get him on the phone all morning — no reply. When I walked Woss, I dropped in on the Thicket Arms Inn, asked for him there. They said he left last night. Packed up his suitcase, paid his bill and drove off."

Harriet felt herself going faint. This whole situation seemed so unreal, like something out of a waking nightmare. She wondered if she wasn't back in bed, if Maximilian wasn't lying on top of her duvet as she slept soundly, dreaming horrible things. "Haven't you . . . ?"

Bella rose. She came around to Harriet and took hold of her hand. "Sit — sit with us."

It seemed the most unnatural thing in the world for Harriet to sit and pretend everything was all right . . . as if everything was the same as it had been the previous day . . . but she did as she was told.

Like the others, she stared at the letter in the middle of the table until Robert turned to her and said, "I think you should be the one to open it."

"Me?" Harriet replied. "Why me?"

Bella shrugged. "Why not?"

Harriet realised she had no answer. It was true she was just as much a part of Humble as the rest of them were. Perhaps this was some sort of reward she had been bestowed in celebration of making her first deal.

Some celebration.

Hands trembling, she reached for the envelope, tugging it towards her. She looked over the address — Molinaar's Cottage, Humble Greetings. Then she turned the envelope over, seeing the stamp, and the familiar initials there:

KA

This was it, then.

Or it was an unfunny prank.

She felt a shudder pass through her body — not just because of the responsibility of opening the envelope, but as her brain processed just what was going on with George. She slit the flap open with her index finger then withdrew the folded-up paper from inside.

She unfolded it, and turned her eyes to the handwritten note within, and read aloud:

"Dear Humble,

I am very pleased to ask that we meet for a final round of discussions ahead of my decision on whether or not to proceed. Don't worry about making a return trip to Scotland — I would be most pleased to meet with you in Normonswold. I believe the Thicket Arms Inn is the best place for a visitor? All being well with my schedule, I expect to arrive in the next few days.

Respectfully yours,

Kareema"

The kitchen was awash with a heavier silence than before.

Then Robert said, "Doesn't she state the time and date of her arrival?"

Because it seemed the natural thing to do, Harriet, Bella and Cassandra all set about cleaning the cottage from top to bottom. Although Robert had made agreeable noises about helping them with their task, he had — in reality — become distracted once he had finished polishing the kitchen table, going off muttering to himself before sitting down in his office with his laptop propped before him, tapping away at the keyboard while he frowned at the screen. She supposed they were all dealing with the news in their own way.

Harriet attempted to call George several times, but could get nothing but his voicemail. His phone was switched off. She wondered how many times in his professional life George had actually switched his phone off — and just what it might mean.

Had he decided to return to Australia?

Was he gone from her life forever?

She recalled all of those cautionary tales she had overheard during innumerable parties given by Indigo Miles at Ebbendevor. All those stories about men who had just one day upped and left.

No explanation.

Just walking out the door and never coming back.

The purpose of telling those stories was to show — once and for all — that men — *all men* — were as slippery as snakes. That they weren't to be trusted an inch.

Was this Harriet's own personal cautionary tale?

They finished cleaning around mid-afternoon. With all the windows thrown open, and the glorious sun streaming into the cottage, Bella laid a hand on Cassandra's shoulder, reassuring her there was simply no way she was going to get a minute, worn-in speck off one of the bedroom windows. And now there was nothing else to do about the house, Harriet was on the brink of suggesting that they turn their attentions to the garden. But she realised that the gardener had come by a few days ago, and every-thing looked perfect.

Led by Bella, they descended to the living room, where Bella soon made her excuses and popped off to the kitchen to make a large pitcher of lemonade.

This left Cassandra and Harriet alone.

As the two of them sat in their respective armchairs, the patio windows thrown wide open so the warm air wafted in, Harriet watched Woss lope past the doorway, ears pricked, eyes wide, trying to fathom just what was going on in the human domain.

When Harriet attempted to make eye contact with Cassandra, she only smiled politely and then looked away. Everyone was so busy with their preparations for Kareema's arrival that there had been no time to address the issue of George's disappearance.

Harriet, though, was unperturbed. "Do you think he's really gone for good?"

"Who?"

Harriet rolled her eyes. "George."

"Oh, I . . . I don't know . . ."

"Yes, but what do you feel?"

"What do I feel?"

"Do you think he's gone for good — that he won't come back?"

Cassandra stared back, fright in her eyes. She was clearly looking for some means of escape — perhaps wishing with all her might that Bella might appear in the doorway and call her away for any reason at all. "Oh, I'm not sure . . ."

"I know you're not sure," Harriet replied, through gritted teeth. "But given how well you know him, do you think he'll be back?"

"I . . . uh, *yes.*"

"He'll be back?"

Cassandra was close to tears now. "I think so."

Harriet allowed herself to fall back into an armchair. She propped her elbows up on the arms and stared at the wallpaper. As with every room of the cottage, there were several framed designs of greetings cards that Cassandra and Bella had designed. She enjoyed those almost childlike doodles, and the joyful, everyday scenarios depicted in them — it made her think that life was simple. That there was really no secret to it.

"Thank you," Harriet replied, finally.

30

PREMATURE CELEBRATIONS

*T*here being no other pressing business at Humble once they had opened the letter and cleaned the cottage from top to bottom, Harriet returned home, where she was a touch put out to discover Aunt Adiema and Dorothy waiting for her in the kitchen.

She wanted — more than anything — to skirt the conversation and head right up to bed. But it seemed an impossible proposition. Already, just by stepping through the door, she had seemed to have taken centre stage. Even Maximilian took his opportunity to twist around her calves. She bent down and scooped him into her arms, at least able to enjoy his fuzzy body and the unstoppable *purrs* rumbling through her chest. She looked to Aunt Adiema and Dorothy — each of them had a chilled glass of water before them, and Dorothy was wearing his suit, tie hanging loose from his unbutton shirt, apparently having just got back from the office.

It was Dorothy who spoke first. "We heard about George — that he skipped town."

Harriet was unbelieving at first, thinking Dorothy was being insensitive in his treatment of such a delicate matter. And then she reminded herself he was always like that — somewhat unsqueemish about dealing with tricky issues. Wasn't this better than having to drag up what everybody was thinking as she had had to do at Humble with Cassandra?

From somewhere, Harriet managed to find a smile. "You haven't seen him . . . *somewhere*, have you?"

Aunt Adiema glanced across the table to Dorothy, and then back to her. "No, dear, we're afraid not."

Harriet squeezed Maximilian tighter, feeling his purrs getting stronger and stronger, coming in waves. And then, as Harriet thought she was becoming faint, that she was going to have to make her excuses and go and lie down for half an hour, Maximilian squirmed in her arms and broke free, leaping down onto the kitchen floor.

As she watched him go, she realised she must've been squeezing him a little too tightly. She was infinitely glad she wasn't handling any sort of heavy machinery.

"Sit," Aunt Adiema said, indicating a chair.

Harriet held off, not wanting to commit herself. She just wanted to be alone. She was tired of being around other people. She hated it when they ignored the situation with George, and it was painful to be forced into speaking about it, too.

But her aunt still held some sort of maternal authority over her, and so she took her place at the table, feeling as if she was immediately pinned beneath Aunt Adiema and Dorothy's joint stare.

"We heard you've had some good news today," Dorothy said.

"What?" And then Harriet recalled the letter. She managed to raise a smile from somewhere. "Yeah, well, I suppose we'll see. Kareema wants to come down here, to Normonswold, for a final round of discussions. Nothing's been promised or signed or anything like that, so we're trying not to get our hopes up too much."

Aunt Adiema grinned. "That sounds like Robert speaking, to me."

"Yeah, he wanted to impress upon us all that nothing has been done yet. That we need to keep on working on the deal. That we can't expect Kareema to do what we want simply because she's going out of her way to meet us here."

"It sounds good to me," Dorothy said. "Almost cause for cele-bration, actually." And, with that, he crossed the kitchen, opened the fridge, and withdrew a bottle of champagne. He paused a moment, looking around their faces, and then sent the cork pinging off the ceiling. Champaign foamed forth from the bottle, spewing down the sides. "Quick! Glasses!"

Harriet mobilised at the same time as Aunt Adiema, the two of them making for the cabinet which contained the champagne flutes. Between the two of them, they managed to extract three glasses, and not before time as more and more champagne slopped onto the kitchen tiles at their feet.

Once they all bore a glass, Dorothy made a toast. "In celebra-tion of our dearest Harriet, who might be going through some awfully awkward business, but who shall surely come out the other side smelling of roses." And then he held up his glass and tipped the contents down his throat. As Harriet suckled at her own glass, she couldn't help but think there was simply no way Dorothy would be able to wear the same suit to work tomorrow given the amount of champagne he had spilled over it this evening.

Once they had finished the toast — if not the entire bottle of champagne — Harriet yawned several times and then made her excuses. When she got up to her bedroom, she saw that Maximilian was spread out there. He purred away when he saw her, apparently having forgiven or forgotten her rough-handed treatment earlier.

Harriet was dozing when she heard her mobile phone buzz away on her bedside table. She looked at it, seeing the screen was illuminated. That it was George calling. Although everything within her screamed out for her to pick up the phone and answer the call, she managed to hold back.

He had made his decision . . . apparently.

As she watched the screen, she saw the voicemail notification blink up.

She hesitated another few seconds, and then reached out for the phone.

As she listened to the robotic woman in her voicemail, she stared out of the window to the sun setting over Normonswold. It was such a beautiful day. She thought about how wonderful it would've been for her and George to take a walk outside together.

Hearing George's voice in her ear, she turned her full attention back to the phone.

"Hi, Harriet. It's me." He took a deep breath. "I'm . . . sorry that things have happened this way, but I have my reasons. I hope you can understand. For what it's worth, I believe that you have what it takes to fulfil whatever role Bella eventually assigns you at Humble. I really think that it's a marvellous opportunity. You just need to have confidence in your own ability and you can do just about anything at all." There was a long pause, and Harriet wondered if the voicemail reel wasn't going to run out. Then he went on, "I won't be in touch for a while. It doesn't seem fair, now that I've done this. I suppose I've made my decision." He paused another few seconds, then added, "Well, goodbye," and hung up.

Harriet stared at the ceiling, trying to fathom just what this phone call had meant. From the sounds of what she'd heard, George already seemed to be regretting having done what he'd done. Had she really interpreted that correctly?

Harriet thought she might feel angry, or out of her mind with despair. But, in actual fact, she felt almost entirely neutral — unperturbed by what George had said.

It was only when she turned over in bed and closed her eyes — with Maximilian purring away against her calves —that she realised she was crying.

A MILITARY OPERATION

*H*arriet was surprised when — during the meeting the next day — it was decided she would be given full responsibility for Kareema's hospitality in Normonswold. Bella, George and Cassandra already had enough daily duties to keep them occupied during daylight hours.

They had placed their trust in her.

Responsibility weighed on her shoulders.

Still, Harriet supposed it was a welcome distraction — something to keep her mind off George, and how he had walked out on them. How he had walked out on *her*.

It seemed obvious Harriet's first stop should be to the Thicket Arms Inn. Even as she crossed the threshold, she couldn't help but feel the place would be woefully inadequate for someone of Kareema Ashburton's standing. Then again, she supposed just about any place at all would be 'inadequate' for someone who had their own *castle*.

The reception area featured several local birds stuffed and

arranged in glass presentation boxes. She felt their beady eyes upon her as she cast a critical eye over the old-time reception area, complete with its large, round service bell and patterned wallpaper.

She gave the bell a tap, and the resulting sound brought Frieda Smyth scurrying out through the beaded curtains which separated the back room from the reception area.

With her glasses perched on the end of her nose, she scrutinised Harriet, as if she had never seen her before in her life.

"Yes?" Frieda said.

"I'm . . . uh, looking to make a reservation . . ."

Frieda arched an eyebrow and frowned. "This isn't a *motel*, you realise?"

Harriet flushed. She had forgotten how severe Frieda was. "It's not for me — it's for a visitor."

"I see."

Harriet felt her heart beating hard against the underside of her throat. She had the urge to leave. But there was nowhere else nearby for Kareema Ashburton to stay. Unless Kareema stayed at her aunt's house, or at Molinaar's Cottage itself. And neither of those seemed to be satisfying solutions.

"Can I . . . see one of the rooms?"

Frieda glared at her over the desk, as if the rooms at the Thicket Arms would be anything short of exemplary. With a shrug and a sigh, Frieda turned her back on Harriet, snatched one of the dangling keys off its hook, and then stormed her way off in the direction of the staircase.

Several heartbeats later Harriet realised she was supposed to follow.

"Not had much business this year," Frieda said, clinging to the handrail as she trod up the stairs. "Just got the one room ready for visitors."

The manner in which Frieda made these statements made it seem as if it was singularly Harriet's fault. "I'm sure things will pick up soon."

"Humph, not now we're headed into autumn. *Nobody* visits in autumn."

Genuinely having nothing to say to this, Harriet stared on up ahead, following on Frieda's — thankfully swift — heels.

It was strange to think that Harriet had lived in Normonswold for so many years — visited the pub at the Thicket Arms so many times — and yet she had never once visited the hotel part of the operation. She was, of course, well-acquainted with Frieda Smyth, and her sour manner. There were many theories about town which attempted to explain Frieda's unhappy attitude to life. One of them spoke of her as being widowed, and never remarrying, and this being what had gradually turned her bitter over the course of the years. And then there were others which claimed she had never married but had in fact suffered some childhood trauma from which she had never fully recovered. The only thing which concerned Harriet about Frieda was whether — if she remained in Normonswold alone, as a single woman — she would turn out the same after a few decades.

There was something for her to look forward to . . .

The room was about what Harriet had expected, which as to say that it delivered nothing that the reception area hadn't promised. She supposed she should have been thankful that there were no stuffed birds in glass boxes.

There was, however, a trio of sombre-looking, sepia-tinted

sketches, depicting Normonswold and its various features, all draped in a glum, perpetual fog.

There was a framed drawing of the forests, and another of the view of the village from down near the river bank. And then there was a further drawing still which depicted the main street — the cobblestones all sheening with dew.

Harriet attempted to overlook the sketches — and the patterned wallpaper — turning her attention instead onto the far more important matter of the bed.

She saw it was neat and tidy, made up already. There was a white bath towel folded at the foot, and the bedside table was left orderly.

Frieda sighed. "Guest just left this morning. Not had the chance to change the bedsheets, or the towels, or whatever." She shook her head at the sight. "Must've been a neat-freak, or something. Never get why people bother to make their bed and fold their towels when we've got to wash everything anyway."

Harriet felt her heart drop to her stomach. George had stayed here. It changed everything about the room to *know* he had been here. That he had passed so many *hours* here.

Harriet looked to Frieda, and then, seeing she was currently inspecting a broken fingernail, she trod off into the bathroom.

Well, it was certainly nothing to compare with the bathroom she had shared with George back at the castle, but she supposed it would have to do. She hoped Kareema Ashburton didn't mind things a little folksy and ragged.

Then the thought struck. She returned to the bedroom.

Frieda Smyth was staring out of the window and tapping her foot impatiently.

"Uh, we're going to need another room," Harriet said.

"Are you?" Frieda replied, without enthusiasm.

"There are two people coming to stay."

Frieda breathed in deeply, sighed out hard, and then trod out of the bedroom, as if this was any sort of response.

Harriet gave the room one final lookover — felt her heart twisting again as she pictured George packing up his suitcase that morning to leave Normonswold forever — and then she headed out after Frieda.

32

MEASURING UP

*T*he next few days were tense. Many times, Harriet wondered whether Kareema hadn't had some kind of malicious intent in refusing to give them an exact date for her visit.

It was almost as if she wanted to catch them out.

That she wanted to see them in their 'natural' habitat, whatever that really meant.

Harriet didn't need to discuss the matter with Bella or Robert to know that she was just being foolish, however, and that Kareema was a very busy woman who couldn't account for what she might have going on one day to the next. When the phone call finally did come, it was at the worst possible time.

That morning, Harriet had spoken with a distributor in the city, who had informed her that they hadn't received this month's delivery. Harriet had gone through the whole rigmarole of calling around to everyone who might be responsible, attempting to ascertain where the slipup had occurred. When she answered the phone next, she was expecting there to be some manager on the other end ready to give her an explanation.

Instead, though, it was Sylvie.

Kareema's personal assistant . . . and doctor.

"Hello, Harriet," Sylvie said, her voice set at a *purr*.

Although Harriet was sure Sylvie meant to imply nothing in her tone, she couldn't help but think there was a slightly gloating edge to her greeting. As if she appreciated and savoured the panic that one of Kareema Ashburton's visits secured upon the hosts.

"Uh, hi," Harriet managed to get out, sliding the notes she'd been making about the misplaced delivery to one side. She looked about the kitchen, half expecting to see Robert or Bella or Cassandra standing in the doorway. But nobody else seemed to be around.

"We'll be arriving in the next hour. Will you be able to meet us?"

"Uh, yes . . . yes, I will."

"Good," Sylvie replied. "Then we shall see you shortly."

Harriet sat at the kitchen table, staring at the wall, the phone still pressed to the side of her head. When she saw something move out of the corner of her eye, she almost leaped out of her skin. Her heart hammering against her ribs, she brought her vision into focus, realising it was Woss; that he had risen from his bed in the corner where he'd been sleeping. He cocked his head with incomprehension at Harriet and then trudged out of the kitchen.

Harriet drew in steady, deep breaths.

But she felt like the whole world was rapidly spinning out of control.

Harriet busied herself getting ready. It was almost impossible to keep her thoughts straight — to keep her mind on task for anything than a matter of seconds. She had roused Bella, Robert and Cassandra at once, of course, and it had hardly helped that they had all entered full-on panic mode too. She wondered at how ridiculous they might all seem to someone who had a hidden camera recording the goings-on at Molinaar's Cottage — all of them losing their minds, like a group of ants whose hill had caught fire.

The disorientating effect was increased as Bella got out the vacuum cleaner — apparently not content with the state of the cottage — and began to work her way from top to bottom. Robert, meanwhile, plodded about the house cradling his laptop in one arm while tapping away at the keyboard with the other hand. When Harriet searched for Cassandra, she located her in the front room of the cottage, putting the last touches to some of her sketches. She looked up at Harriet when she came in and smiled unconvincingly. "Do you think this looks all right?"

Harriet came closer and looked over Cassandra's shoulder. She saw that Cassandra had created a breath-taking sketch of Broidersbarth — Kareema Ashburton's castle. It was exactly how Harriet remembered it. "Did you do this from a photo?"

"No," Cassandra replied, flushing slightly. "It's all from memory. There wasn't really any time for photos."

"It's . . . wonderful. Is it a gift for Kareema?"

"That's the plan."

Harriet said nothing more, wondering just what George might say to Cassandra about such a plan. He always had something to say whenever one of them suggested something like this — it would most likely be 'out of place', or the 'wrong sort of gesture' . . . but George wasn't here any longer.

After about half an hour, the nervous energy within the cottage reached a simmering point. Each of them in their own time seemed to acknowledge that there was nothing else to be done about the house, so they all took to waiting at the kitchen table — no cups of tea in front of them this time.

The room was so silent Harriet could hear the *tick-tick-tick* of the kitchen clock. And she could hear Woss's gentle panting as he calmed himself down after having loped about the house excitedly, getting under everybody's feet, though clearly trying to help out.

When there was a knock at the door, everybody sat still at the kitchen table.

It was as if Death himself had come calling.

Then, as if it couldn't be any other way, Harriet rose from her chair and went to the door. She took a deep breath and then opened up.

Standing there, on the front step, was Kareema Ashburton, Sylvie, and — lagging a little way further back along the garden path — George.

Harriet's heart swelled in her throat. Then it pounded in her chest.

She thought she might scream, but she held herself calm, brought Kareema and Sylvie into focus, and concentrated on them. "Won't you please come in?"

33

AN IDIOT INSIDE

*G*eorge had to admit he felt like a prize fool to be entering Molinaar's Cottage on Kareema and Sylvie's coattails. He had felt like more of an idiot earlier that day, though.

It had been around eight o'clock this morning — about an hour after he had woken up — that he had had the revelation. That he had made a great mistake in leaving Normonswold behind. And that he had meant what he had said to Harriet.

That he loved her.

For him, there had been no choice but to get in his car and to drive back.

During the course of the past few weeks, he had convinced himself the injuries he had sustained in the gym at Kareema's castle were getting better — that he was on the mend. Not wanting to lose his svelte figure, he had returned to some light running. He had been surprised at just how well his body had held up. He was able to manage the pain with a couple of tablets before workouts and then a few more afterwards. Already he had felt the mental benefits of returning to an exercise routine. He felt fresher, happier, his mind clearer.

He had only to jump in his car — he had only to return.

Nothing to it.

It seemed so simple.

And so it had played out, as he had swooped out of the city and onto the motorway. But it had been the point when he had entered the labyrinthine country roads leading to Normonswold when he had felt the twitching start.

The sensation had begun as nothing more than an itch in his side. Nothing more than a minor annoyance. It had come on as he had turned a particularly sharp corner, perhaps going ten miles an hour faster than he really needed to. He had almost lost control of the car then, feeling the eerie tingling feeling passing over the surface of his skin.

Wincing, he had managed to stay on track, though . . . at least until the next bend.

Anticipating the sensation coming on again, he had gripped the steering wheel more tightly, determined not to lose control another time. He had slowed as much as he could, and then, approaching the bend, carefully turned the steering wheel.

Halfway through the turn, he had realised he couldn't take it any longer. The tingling had given way to pain, and he had felt a burning sensation take hold of his ribs. It was a miracle he managed to get all the way through the turn without dragging his car into a ditch. He had seen sense then — his body had *made* him see sense — as wave-upon-wave of pain had set upon him, relentless. As he had sat parked up at the side of the country road, on his way to Normonswold, he had told himself he would call for someone to come and recover his car, and he would get a lift back into the village. But when he had reached for his phone, the battery was flat. He supposed he hadn't been thinking as clearly as he had believed. He always left his phone to charge overnight.

As he had sat behind the wheel, feeling pain ripple through him, he had started to believe he deserved nothing less. He had been the one who had walked away from Normonswold, from Humble . . . albeit he had had his reasons, but that was no excuse. Even though it perturbed him to think what might happen to him — and his sense of worth — if Kareema decided to veto the deal, he told himself he would just need to take it in his stride.

And that decision had seemed far nobler when he had been back in his flat in the city, and not right here, parked up at the side of the road.

It had been then that he had noticed a car approaching, in the rear-view mirror. He had taken stock of the four-by-four shape, and how the car had tinted windows. It made him think that someone from the Secret Service had come to take him away.

Because he could think of nothing else to do — and because he was worried he might end up waiting at the side of the road until nightfall if he didn't — he stuck his arm out of the window, signalling the approaching car.

When the car pulled up behind him, and the familiar figure of Sylvie stepped down from the driver's side, he had felt the pain overtake him again.

Locking every nerve in his body.

It was as if just the sight of Sylvie had brought all his fears back. That he could *fail* . . . that he could be found wanting. He had wondered what he was going to say — he wondered if he should just smile, claim he had made a mistake, and allow them to drive on to Normonswold . . . to leave him here, at the side of the road, for someone else to come along in the other direction, headed back to the city.

Maybe that was his destiny, after all.

But somehow, and perhaps it was testament to the love he felt for Harriet, he had agreed to Sylvie's offer for a lift, and he returned with them, to Normonswold.

To Molinaar's Cottage.

To Harriet.

34

LOADED DICE

*H*arriet wasn't quite sure what to do with her hands or —for that matter — any part of her body. She greeted Kareema Ashburton with a kiss on either cheek, and then repeated the same gesture with Sylvie. It was only when George arrived, limping on their heels, that she felt her gut swelling. He had a visceral effect on her. As if he had invisible hands which could influence her thoughts and feelings — which could reach out and manipulate her to his will. She did her best to hold still. The best she managed was a nod to George, before she backed away, more out of a sense of wanting to accommodate Kareema and Sylvie than for any other reason.

Harriet immediately made herself busy, going about making tea for Kareema and Sylvie. Whenever she glanced back over her shoulder, it seemed surreal to see the pair of women here. They had spent so long anticipating their visit that they had taken on a kind of mythological state, as if they had never even really existed at all — as if they had never been to visit Kareema's Scottish castle.

She half expected George to help her, for him to take the opportunity to sidle up alongside her and apologise for what he had done.

What would she be able to say to him with Kareema and Sylvie in the room?

She was glad he had decorum enough — even if it was a sense of professional pride over all else — so as not to make a scene in the kitchen.

They could talk about this later.

Or so Harriet convinced herself.

She brought the tea over to the kitchen table, handing a mug to Kareema and to Sylvie, and thinking about just how *inadequate* this must seem — the two of them used to a battery of servants waiting upon them. Then again, she hoped it might count in their favour. Perhaps the fact Humble did not yet employ a butler might hit home with Kareema that this was a responsible start-up. One which wasn't accustomed to frivolous spending.

Harriet allowed herself to drift into the background as Bella and Robert made polite conversation. Cassandra took her place alongside Harriet, and Woss pressed himself up against Harriet's calves, clearly wanting to stay out of trouble. George took up a seat on the other side of the kitchen, not quite at the table — not quite *part* of the meeting.

She wondered just what steps Robert had taken with respect to George, whether or not he was even officially part of the business any longer.

When Kareema and Sylvie finished their tea, Bella offered them a tour of the house.

Not wanting to crowd them, the others all held back.

An uncomfortable silence draped over the kitchen, and — as they listened to Bella, Kareema and Sylvie treading their way upstairs — it was George who decided to break it.

"I just want to say how sorry I am — just wanted to admit how much of an *idiot* I've been. Leaving this place, leaving Humble, was nothing short of the most stupid, most cowardly thing I have done in my entire life."

George looked to them all, locking eyes with Robert for the longest time.

Harriet knew well that attempting to elicit emotions in Robert where business was concerned was a Very Dangerous Thing Indeed . . . but, then again, she supposed that if anybody had any chance of making a success of such a technique then it was George.

George switched his attention onto Harriet, and she felt as if she was sinking into the kitchen tiles. She wanted to tell him to look someplace else — to tell him that they could speak about things later on; about their relationship, or whatever it was that they had had . . . about how they had said that they *loved* one another . . .

"Harriet, will you ever forgive me?"

Harriet felt everybody's eyes upon her. Although she didn't dare break away from George's gaze, she thought that even Woss was staring at her, waiting to see what she would say. Thankfully, it was then that Robert and Cassandra exchanged glances. Without a word between them, they left the kitchen, Woss somehow getting the hint and loping along on their heels. Harriet felt her whole body seize up. She did her best not to meet George's eye, knowing it would be an admission of defeat if she did . . . that she would have no grounds to ever claim personal pride ever again . . . but then she looked.

George stepped towards her. His eyes fixed onto hers. It felt as if time itself had slowed. As if the two of them were alone in all of time and space.

She felt her heart beating in her stomach.

Blood throbbed at her temples.

Everything told her she should turn and run. That she should escape the situation. That she should make George suffer for what he had done . . . for — if she didn't — then what might he do in the future? He would know that he was utterly in control.

Forevermore.

And yet, with all of this logic storming about her skull, Harriet found it difficult to see clearly. Logic slipped away from her, quickly becoming irrelevant.

George stood so that only an arm's length separated them. She felt his warm breath up against her cheeks. He smelled so wonderful. Everything about him yearned for her to reach out and touch. But she needed to resist.

Continuing to stare into her eyes, he began to close on her.

A flicker of electricity passed through Harriet's nerves.

Then a twitching sensation up her spine.

Before he could gain the upper hand, she decided to seize it. She lurched forwards, grabbing him by the back of the neck and plunging their mouths together.

As they kissed, she explored his back, feeling the well-developed muscles surrounding his shoulders. She told herself to be tender, but it was difficult with all the feelings flowing through her. She told herself he was damaged, that he was still recovering from the gym session back at Kareema's castle, and yet she found it difficult to hold herself back.

Impossible, in fact.

As they embraced, Harriet felt George wince slightly as her hands explored further down his back. But she only clung on tighter — refusing to let him go. He was the one who had come back to her. He would be the one to suffer the consequences.

The sound of approaching voices brought Harriet back to the present.

She eased herself apart from George, almost unwilling to allow him free from her arms. But now was the time for business.

Now it was time for them to earn their bread.

35

DUE DILIGENCE

*H*arriet had to admit that — at least from the looks on Kareema and Sylvie's faces — it seemed things were going well. If she had been an uninterested outsider, looking on at the scene, she might even have assumed they were all extended family members from the way everybody was smiling. They all seemed at ease in one another's company.

Bella turned her attention onto Harriet. And Harriet was certain she was wrong, that she had somehow mistaken her for Cassandra; because surely Cassandra was the one who Kareema and Sylvie would be most concerned with.

It was then that Harriet noticed Kareema held the framed sketch of her castle — Broidersbarth — that Cassandra had drawn.

Did this mean that Cassandra's shift was over?

That she had done her part of looking after Kareema?

"We were going to take a trip to the woods," Bella said. "Kareema doesn't want to go, so we were wondering if you'd like to show her your aunt's stables?"

Harriet felt her chest tighten. "My aunt's stables?"

"Yeah," Bella said, still smiling, but now with a slight sense of mania lurking in her tone of voice, behind the toothy grin.

Realising Kareema was looking at her, waiting for the response, Harriet snapped back to reality. She had only to think of the hospitality Kareema had offered them in Broidersbarth. Was there any way Harriet could deny her anything?

And then there was the small factor of *knowing* that anything she might directly — or indirectly — do could affect the outcome of the deal.

The outcome of Humble.

Whether or not they really took off or remained as they were . .
.

She had Bella's dreams in her hands.

Harriet forced a smile, looked to Kareema, and tried to ignore the squirming feeling in her gut. "Sure," she said.

"Great," Bella replied, and then looked to Robert, Cassandra and Sylvie. "We'll all pile into the car, then. Shouldn't be longer than about an hour — it's going to be dark soon."

And, with that, Harriet stood still, feeling very much like a boulder in the middle of a fast-moving river. She watched on as Woss trotted on Robert's heels, following the others out of Molinaar's Cottage.

Once the voices had floated out of the front door, and a little way down the path, Harriet returned to the present. She looked to George, suddenly delighted he was here with her. The smile on her lips now felt more of an authentic expression of her true feelings. It was easier when she had no need to fake emotion.

She looked to Kareema. "Come on," she said. "It's just a short walk up the road."

"This really is a lovely little village."

Harriet looked to Kareema, who was drinking her surroundings in with a genuine sense of glee. They stopped in at the Thicket Arms Inn so Kareema might drop off the framed sketch of Broidersbarth which Cassandra had given her. Since the others had taken the car to the woods, there was nowhere else for Kareema to leave it for the time being.

When they reached the Thicket Arms, Harriet had every intention of approaching Frieda at the reception desk, but Kareema beat her to it.

Harriet slipped George a glance, knowing since he had spent a good deal of time at the hotel, he would understand the peril they were getting themselves in for.

However, Harriet was rendered surprised as she watched Frieda break out in a grisly grin. "Ms Ashburton, I suppose?"

Kareema smiled back at her pleasantly.

Harriet supposed Kareema was used to being recognised all over the place, and that it wouldn't be so strange for someone to know who she was even in a backwater town such as this one. "That's right," Kareema replied.

"You did some business with my brother, many years ago now."

"I see."

Frieda was nodding away. "He was in the carpet trade. You might remember him. Anders Smyth?"

"I do."

Harriet was surprised at the sharpness of Kareema's response. As if her brain was nothing more than a computerised database, and she could recall names from it without so much as batting an eyelid.

"You helped him to reach . . . well, the *entire* world." Frieda looked past Kareema, over her shoulder to George and Harriet. Although Harriet half expected Frieda's smile to slacken, it remained as sharp as ever. Frieda turned her attention back to Kareema. "He made an absolute fortune. He was able to help me .. . back when things were a little sticky — when I was having some financial issues."

"I am glad."

Harriet waited for Kareema to add something else. It seemed almost as if she should bring Kareema up to date about how Frieda Smyth usually acted — tell her she was never this fawning, or went out of her way to be kind in any way.

"He, uh, passed away a few years ago now," Frieda said.

"I am sorry to hear that." Kareema allowed a moment's pause, and then held out the framed sketch of Broidersbarth. "I just wanted to leave this with you, if that's all right?"

Frieda stared at the sketch for the longest time. And then — without warning — a tear snaked its way down her cheek. Flushing now, she blinked rapidly, then reached up and wiped her face. "I shall keep it safe," she said, taking it and turning her back on them with a quick smile. "See you later, Ms Ashburton. I hope you enjoy Normonswold, and please let me know if there is anything — *anything at all* — that I can do for you."

On their way out of the reception area of the Thicket Arms, Harriet noticed something she hadn't done on her previous visit. But, then again, why would she? There was a whole wall of pictures hanging there. Now, though, one in particular caught her attention. Walking slowly, on Kareema and George's heels, she took note of a sepia-stained photograph. It had to have been taken thirty or forty years ago. There was no mistaking the subject, though.

It was Broidersbarth.

In the bottom corner, there was a handwritten note in silver ink. As Harriet trod her way out of the door, she just managed to make out the message:

With many thanks for your visit.
Best wishes,
Kareema

They were already knocking on the front door when the idea of contacting Aunt Adiema ahead of time occurred to Harriet. But, as she heard her aunt's unmistakable, heavy gait within, she realised it was a bit late to be thinking of advanced notifications.

To tell the truth, Harriet was surprised her aunt was at home at all — it was strange to see her aunt around her house during the day and not at the stables themselves.

The door swung open. Her aunt was just as she had always appeared in Harriet's mind's eye: dressed in jodhpurs, knee-high riding boots, a riding crop dangling from her fingers.

Aunt Adiema took a moment to appraise the situation and then she broke out in a wide smile. "Why, Kareema, isn't it?"

"Yes, that's right."

As always, Adiema was somewhat clumsy in the way she simultaneously attempted to shake hands and take a step forward. But Kareema seemed unaffected by her lack of grace.

The greeting done with, Adiema sat back on her heels, as if working out the situation. And then she said, "I suppose you've come to see the stables?"

"Yes, auntie."

"All right, all right!" Adiema thrust a finger up in the air, and then disappeared back into the front hall of the house another moment.

She emerged clutching a bundle of keys.

Right as she brought the door shut behind her, Maximilian just managed to slither out through the crack. Harriet supposed some feline sense of curiosity had roused him from his nap, prompting him to investigate just what was going on around his territory.

With Maximilian striding along ahead — apparently knowing just where they were going — they headed for the stables. Adiema showed them where she kept the horses, introducing Kareema to each one of them by name, and then answering all of Kareema's follow-up questions about their diets and habits with enthusiasm.

When it came to anything of an equine matter, Adiema had no cause to affect enthusiasm. When the inevitable question came around — whether or not Kareema would like to take a ride — Harriet fully expected Kareema to handle the question in the same manner other polite visitors to the Adiema Smith Riding School did, which was to blush slightly, thank Adiema for the opportunity, and turn it down.

Harriet was stunned when Kareema took Adiema up on her offer.

Clearly surprised herself that someone had taken up her offer, Adiema set about tacking up a pony called Jim. He was an old, faithful horse, who Adiema would often give to nervous, first-time riders. Harriet had ridden Jim the half dozen times Adiema had actually managed to get her on a horse.

Harriet, George, and Maximillian all paced along behind Kareema — in the saddle — as Adiema led Jim in front of them to the practice paddock. The paddock was scattered with golden sands. Just as it always was. Adiema employed one of her neighbour's sons, a young boy who came by every morning to rake the sand, make it neat and tidy, before he headed to school. Although Harriet was unsure of the exact arrangement Adiema had struck with the boy, she had her suspicions that the pay wasn't lucrative . . . but the boy was faithful in his dedication and consistency whatever the meagre compensation.

Harriet and George held back at the wooden fences, choosing to watch on as Adiema took up her place in the middle of the paddock, allowing Jim some slack on the long rope she had him attached to. Kareema's white hair streamed behind her from beneath the helmet she had been given. When Harriet studied Kareema's face, she saw a kind of girlish enthusiasm there. Flushed cheeks and a sense of wonder glimmering in her eye. Perhaps Bella had missed a trick in hiring Harriet and not her Aunt Adiema.

After Kareema had rounded the ring for the first time, Harriet felt George's gentle touch on the back of her hand. It sent a shiver up her spine. Although she knew she shouldn't allow him back into her favours so easily, there was also something elemental — something *fundamental* — which made her want to reach for him naturally.

Which made her want to hold him.

To run her hands over his muscles.

And to feel his warmth beside her own.

Before Harriet could quite control herself, she took hold of his hand and squeezed. There was no denying that she was greatly happy that he was back. That she *had* him back.

This was his last chance.

And Harriet was determined to make it the last one he needed.

The session continued for the best part of half an hour. Harriet said nothing to George, and George said nothing to her. She enjoyed the gentle silence which fell between them. It seemed natural. As if there was nothing more worthwhile for them to say.

When Harriet noticed Adiema was reeling in the leading rope, and that Jim's circles about the paddock were becoming tighter and tighter, she prepared herself to turn back on her charm for Kareema. She glanced to George, then scolded herself for believing she should look to him for approval.

He had apologised.

And Harriet knew that it was up to her to make her own decisions about how she should or should not act.

Harriet found it impossible to take her eyes off Adiema and Kareema as they approached. It was difficult to tell which one of them was smiling more widely. Harriet felt herself grinning too. As was George.

Feeling Maximilian winding around her calves, Harriet bent down and scooped him up. He purred against her chest as she squeezed him tightly.

Everything seemed so perfect, and the sun was shining so brightly.

And then disaster struck.

Harriet saw everything play out in slow motion — and yet there was no time.

No time at all.

Kareema's smile remained just as wide — perhaps growing wider still — but her eyelids . . . they began to droop. And then they closed completely.

Almost as if Kareema had fallen asleep.

Harriet leaped off her mark, her reflexes ahead of her conscious thought.

She took a step.

Two.

Every one of her actions took so long.

And then she was suddenly alongside the horse.

Kareema slipped from the saddle.

Harriet reached up her arms, catching her.

And the two of them fell to the ground.

As they lay there, a word rasped between Kareema's lips.

"Sylvie."

HOSPITAL

*E*verything passed so quickly.

Before Harriet knew quite what was happening, she was behind the wheel of George's car — George in the passenger seat — while Adiema was in the back, propping up Kareema Ashburton. Harriet had jabbed the hazard lights and they blinked away as she drove at high speed along the motorway. Only a few months ago, she would've felt as if she was on the brink of losing control. Now, though, she felt as if she had the skills to get them where they needed to go. And she had George beside her. That helped greatly to instil a sense of confidence. Given his injury, he was in no state to drive.

It was up to her.

She drove them on, squeezing the steering wheel so tightly that all the blood seeped out of her knuckles. She felt a single bead of sweat slipping down from her forehead.

"Just here — turn off here," George said.

Harriet did as he said, making for the exit slip road, driving them at high speed away from the rest of the motorway traffic. As she tore across a roundabout, she heard a cacophony of car horns all around her.

They were impossibly loud.

Even a matter of weeks ago — perhaps even under normal circumstances — they would've been enough to throw off her concentration.

But not today.

She was determined to get them where they needed to go.

With an enormous building growing up out of the landscape, she eyed the sprawling car park. It was an overwhelming sight. Even despite the situation — the extreme urgency with which they needed to get Kareema medical care — she couldn't help but think how lucky she had been in her own life. She had always had her health. There had never been anything major which had afflicted her. It was overwhelming to consider the amount of people who streamed into — and hopefully *out of* — hospitals each and every day.

And now Kareema Ashburton was going to be another of their number.

Harriet parked them up in one of the bays.

That done, she rounded the car to open the door.

Kareema was still just about conscious.

She was receptive to Harriet's out held hand, although she felt impossibly frail.

Harriet met Aunt Adiema's eye.

They might've had their differences, but they still shared a sort of telepathic connection. All of those years living together had contributed to the understanding of the other's unspoken cues and hints.

Together, with George lagging on their heels, they headed for the Accident and Emergency Department.

Harriet sat in the plastic chair doing her best to find a comfortable position. But it was impossible. She could hear the constant *tick-tick* of the clock above her head, intermingled with the more furious *clacking* of the receptionist's keyboard. Outside, the sun was setting. It was almost as if she was viewing footage from some other world — from some other time. The fluorescent lightbulbs offered only a kind of dry illumination. It seemed that whereas natural light nourished, this false light exhausted.

She wanted nothing more than to be away from this place.

For Kareema to become well again.

They had passed such a wonderful afternoon.

A *perfect* afternoon.

And then this . . .

It was about twenty minutes after they had arrived that Sylvie came trotting through the doors. Her hair was in a flurry. Her eyes wild. And her blouse untucked. If someone had told her that Sylvie was anything other than completely immaculate in her appearance then she would never have believed them.

But she supposed an episode like this was all it took.

And she couldn't blame her.

Any given person in the whole world was only ever one personal tragedy away from total mania.

Spotting them, Sylvie slowed to a swift walk. "Where is she?"

Harriet took a sharp breath, seeing George and Adiema's dumbstruck faces as they sat beside her. "They took her off into a ward. She's being seen by a doctor."

224

This, though, was apparently not the answer Sylvie was looking for.

She left them behind at great speed.

Turning her attention to the receptionist.

Before Harriet could even blink, Sylvie flew into a wild argument with the receptionist, of which she overheard various snatched fragments. The receptionist refusing to give up information on Kareema's whereabouts. When a member of security approached to intervene, Sylvie sidestepped him, and grabbed hold of a passing doctor — snatching his white coat in her fist. To begin with, the doctor panicked. He attempted to shove Sylvie away. But she clung onto him, and not even the might of the security guard trying to wrestle her free could intervene. Harriet stood up, waiting to rush in, but at the same time knowing that she mustn't — that she would only make the situation worse.

She wondered if she could just get everyone to calm down.

If she could just have a moment to *explain* . . . but things were happening too quickly.

Harriet watched on.

The security guard was winning the battle against Sylvie now, having managed to get her to let go of the doctor. But the doctor, instead of scurrying for safety behind the heavy doors, stood a safe distance back, still listening to what Sylvie said.

And it was then he shifted his attention onto the security guard, telling him to stand down, to let go of Sylvie. After a few moments of reluctance, the security guard did as he was told. He remained at Sylvie's shoulder, though, ready at any second to seize hold of her again if the situation required it.

Sylvie continued to speak with the doctor, making a point of holding her arms down at her sides — of not moving from the spot.

Then the doctor began to nod. He gestured out ahead, to the heavy doors which led deeper into the hospital.

Harriet half expected Sylvie to glance back at them, for her to call them on after her.

When Harriet realised Sylvie wasn't coming back, she took up her seat again — ready to wait with George and Adiema.

About an hour later, Bella, Robert and Cassandra passed through the Emergency Department doors. When Harriet eyed them — set against a charcoal night sky, spotted with only the odd streetlight from the distant town — she felt an almost uncontrollable happiness rising in her chest. It had been such an awful day that she was so glad to see familiar faces.

If Harriet hadn't been rendered ecstatic merely by the sight of the new arrivals, then she would've been by what they carried with them. They had brought a plastic bag full of sandwiches. And although Harriet initially felt nauseous at the idea of eating, she soon changed her mind — realising she was famished.

The six of them all took up their positions, watching over the Accident and Emergency waiting room — each one primed for the news which would surely come soon.

Except it didn't . . .

It was around midnight when Sylvie reappeared.

She was now dressed in a white coat. Her hair looked even more flustered than when she had come in. Her mascara was running. She told them all to go home, get some rest, but they all refused. Under Bella's insistence, Sylvie chewed on one of the sandwiches she had brought. However, Sylvie only got a single bite down before being summoned once more by a doctor, poking his head out around the door which led deeper into the hospital. As the door swung shut behind the two of them, Harriet did her best to see anything beyond.

All she could see was the corridor; lined by many doors.

Kareema could be behind any one of them.

When it got to one in the morning, Robert volunteered to drive back those who wanted to get some rest. Although it wasn't with any small amount of protest, Cassandra and Adiema were eventually persuaded to go along — but only on the assurance that whenever they heard news they were to get in touch immediately.

That left Harriet, Bella and George in the waiting room.

They took turns to nap while the other would sit upright, holding their focus on the door through which Sylvie and the doctor had disappeared. It was on Harriet's watch that Sylvie eventually appeared in the waiting room.

Light had already begun to creep up on the horizon as Harriet got to her feet, forgetting the sleeping Bella and George. It was unnervingly still in the waiting room at this time. There were others there, but they were all dozing too. It was almost as if someone had cast a curse across the land, freezing everybody except Harriet and Sylvie in time.

Sylvie either felt no need to say anything or she simply no longer had the strength. With a nod to Harriet, she invited her in through the door. Harriet shifted a glance at the on-duty receptionist, as if she might need permission, but the receptionist, too, was dozing.

A stench of disinfectant burned Harriet's nostrils. The walls were overpoweringly white, working in combination with the lights to maintain the perpetual illumination. The sandwich she had eaten a few hours ago twisted in her stomach. She felt as if with each and every step she was growing shorter and shorter.

Finally Sylvie brought her to the room — to Kareema's room.

With another nod, Sylvie led her in through the doorway, and to where Kareema lay — now wearing a hospital gown, and propped up in bed with half a dozen pillows. She had several tubes sticking into her, and a series of plastic bags containing multi-coloured liquids which Harriet was unable to identify. The smell of disinfectant was gone here. It took her a long while to place the smell exactly.

In the end she decided it was like breathing in a vat of mechanical grease.

When Kareema turned her head, Harriet flinched.

She had thought she was asleep.

Catching hold of herself — and the situation — Harriet gave herself a mental nudge.

"Hi. How are you doing?"

Kareema murmured something then closed her eyes. When she attempted to open her eyes again, she seemed unable to . . . her eyelids flickering and then giving up the fight.

Sylvie spoke in a low tone. "They've given her a sedative. I managed to convince them not to medicate."

" 'Not to medicate', why?"

Sylvie jerked around, looking to the doorway.

When Harriet turned to look, she saw George and Bella peering in.

Harriet half expected Sylvie to dismiss them right away, however, she strode over, ushered them in, and shut the door behind.

The four of them stood around Kareema's bed.

"Okay," Sylvie said, "what I am about to tell you cannot leave this room, is that clear?"

Harriet looked to George and Bella, seeing the dark bags

clinging to the bottoms of their eyes — eager to help, and yet exhausted.

"We need to get her out of here."

Perhaps if they had been more awake, one of them would've objected.

"And this is how we're going to do it — just watch."

More out of disbelief than anything, the three of them stood back and observed as Sylvie went about disconnecting the various tubes attached to Kareema. She was careful and efficient as she went about it. She left only a single machine hooked up to a spot on Kareema's neck. At this point she turned back around, giving them her full focus.

"When I switch off this machine an alarm will go off in the nurses' station. We will need to move quickly. One minute, two . . . but it won't be long. Then we need to get her out to the car. And we need to be ready to go. Is that clear?"

Harriet's first reaction was to tell Sylvie that no, nothing was clear but she held back.

Maybe she was afraid of bringing up the sandwich she had eaten.

"Right, I need someone to go to the car." Her gaze immediately fell onto Harriet, since she had been the driver.

Harriet felt a fresh surge of heat pass through her stomach.

But she knew she could do this.

She *knew* it.

She nodded. "Fine," she said.

"Now," Sylvie said, looking to George, "you're in no fit state to help with any heavy lifting so you'll be our lookout. If you see someone coming and we're not clear, you'll need to create a diversion. A distraction, okay?"

George prepared to step out into the corridor, but Sylvie held up her hand.

"You need to know something before we go. If you get into any sort of trouble, we can't afford to wait behind. You will face the consequences alone."

"Okay," George replied.

Harriet had the urge to giggle, even despite the serious circumstances. This whole episode was like some sort of military operation. She wondered if Sylvie had been in the Army.

Sylvie shifted to Bella. "You'll need to help me with the lifting, all right?"

"Sure," Bella replied. "Just show me what I need to do."

Sylvie turned back to the bed. She swiftly set about pulling out straps from the sides of the mattress. She passed them over the still-sleeping Kareema. She tugged on the straps several times, making sure they were secure. Then she turned to Harriet.

"Go start the car."

Harriet's heart hardly had a chance to beat more than a dozen times before she was behind the wheel. Morning had broken now, and sunlight flooded everything. There was a soaring blue sky, and it looked as though it was going to be a beautiful day.

She started in one go and brought the car up in front of the Accident and Emergency Department. She felt extremely on edge having parked up in the zone reserved for ambulances only. She peered out through the window with bated breath.

They weren't coming.

She couldn't see them *coming*.

It was only now she realised the security guard — a different one from the other who had been on duty earlier — was pressing his face up against the glass, peering out at her.

He was reaching for his walkie-talkie.

As his lips moved to speak, a soaring shriek filled the air.

It was so loud Harriet thought it was coming from inside the car, but when she looked toward the waiting room, she saw Sylvie and Bella dragging Kareema on the mattress, the two of them bringing her through the automatic doors.

Harriet's attention fell onto the security guard, who was now concentrating on the two women, and the patient they dragged between them. Neither of them so much as looked up at him as he got out of their way, a beleaguered expression on his face.

Harriet snapped into action.

Leaving the car running, she got out and went around to the back seat.

Sylvie and Bella brought the mattress up alongside the car.

Together they lifted Kareema.

Sylvie got into the car first, taking up her position on the far side of the back seat.

Bella helped to ease Kareema in so that her head lay in Sylvie's lap. Then Bella got in, taking care to tuck up Kareema's feet before slamming the door shut behind her.

Harriet got back behind the wheel. Her foot rested on the accelerator, ready to bring it down and send them tearing away, going wherever it was Sylvie was intent they needed to take Kareema. But Harriet couldn't bring her foot down — not yet.

She stared into the Accident and Emergency waiting room, seeing no sign of George.

"Go!" Sylvie shouted from the back seat. "Just *go!*"

Harriet held still, though, unwilling to leave.

She saw movement within the hospital. Guards and porters

had materialised. They were headed for the door through which they had brought Kareema.

The security guard on the doors began to approach.

He brought his walkie-talkie up to his mouth.

Harriet knew it was now or never.

She had to get them out of here.

But not *yet*.

And it was then that she saw him.

George.

He skipped through the now-heavily trafficked waiting room.

Nobody tried to stop him.

And then — almost at the car — the security guard held out his arm.

George was too quick for him, though, diving beneath the outstretched arm and breaking into a sprint for the final few metres.

Harriet inched the car away as George pulled open the passenger-side door and jumped in. She gunned the motor before they had the chance to bask in his glorious escape.

In Kareema's glorious escape.

3 7

IN THE TREES

"Just take us where we went yesterday afternoon," Sylvie said from the back seat.

From the context of what Sylvie was saying, Harriet deduced they were to go to the forests nearby Normonswold. That this was where Sylvie wanted them to be . . . just why they hadn't returned to the village itself, and to the car in which Sylvie and Kareema had arrived, escaped Harriet. If Sylvie was so clear-minded about getting Kareema back home as to break out of hospital, then it seemed odd that she wished for this diversion.

But it wasn't Harriet's job to question.

She just drove.

When they parked up, the sun beaming through the bristling trees, Harriet felt the blood still rushing through her veins. She expected the sound of sirens to break through the tranquil landscape at any given moment. She thought they might have some form of radar tracking them. That a police helicopter would pounce upon them at any given moment.

And yet nothing came.

Nobody was coming . . . or so it seemed.

Harriet and George got out of the car, while Sylvie and Bella helped Kareema out.

It was a miracle Kareema had the strength to stand, albeit with the aid of Sylvie and Bella at either side. Sylvie continued to lead the way, even as she helped Kareema along the path. It appeared she had a destination in mind.

Harriet and George lagged back.

It was easy to think that she had outgrown her usefulness now — that she and George should just go back home and get some rest. But Harriet was determined that Sylvie would be unable to do anything to stop them.

They were coming along whether she liked it or not.

Although it had been difficult to oppose Sylvie during the breakout from the hospital, the utter craziness of what they had just done hit home with her. And she couldn't help thinking that she, George and Bella had something of a duty to keep an eye on her . . . to see exactly what she had planned for Kareema.

They reached the lake, and the cabin alongside it, after a ten-minute walk.

When Bella and Sylvie stopped, Kareema still between them, Harriet had a chance to see the expressions of exertion on their faces. Harriet had wanted to ask them if they wanted any help, but she had been worried about leaving George behind — he had been unable to keep up with the relentless pace of the others, and she had been wary about leaving him behind on the trail, lest the police dogs get him.

Without hesitation, Bella led them up to the cabin, and then through the door.

Inside, there was no need for any sort of light source, the sun simply streamed in through the windows, illuminating everything. They set Kareema down on the camp bed within.

Kareema was breathing shallowly, and her cheeks appeared hollow. Her eyes were slightly open, though, and she was clearly still conscious.

It was then Harriet realised Kareema was attempting to speak, that her lips were moving, but no sound seemed to be making it out. Sylvie ducked her head close to listen.

After about a minute, she straightened up, and asked them to leave.

Harriet felt a moment of resilience, worried about leaving Sylvie alone with Kareema, but when Bella and George moved for the exit, she decided it would be okay as long as they were close by. They could always look in through the windows to see what was happening.

Outside, Harriet allowed herself to breathe in the scent of nuts, and leaves, and soil, and to feel the cooling breeze against her cheeks. The sun warming her hair. It was so wonderful to be out of the hospital — to be out of that utterly unnatural environment.

She looked to Bella and George, and then Bella said something about getting in touch with the others to update them, and left to go around the lake.

Harriet looked to George, staring into his eyes. She felt weariness taking hold of her now — adrenaline fighting a losing battle. She wondered if they would all be marked felons from now on. She wondered if this day marked the end of Humble Greetings; all the key players of the business involved in what had gone on here . . .

She felt for George's hand, entwining his fingers with her own. He squeezed her hand back and then leaned into her, planting a sweet, but dry, kiss upon her lips. She felt as if she might be able to sleep forever after all the events which'd taken place last night.

And yet she had to keep going for a while yet.

She had to stay awake.

Alert.

When Bella returned from her trip around the lake, she gave them a weak smile. "I got in touch with Robert. He roused Cassandra, but it seems like your aunt's out for the count. They won't be long."

A silence fell upon them.

Perhaps it was the strangeness of the situation.

Or that they had all gathered in this particular spot outside Normonswold as if it had all been prearranged.

Harriet looked to the cabin again, seeing Sylvie within. She could see she was speaking with Kareema, although Kareema appeared to only be half conscious.

Something rustled in the trees nearby, and Harriet felt a shudder pass up her spine as she turned back to the others. "Do you think we should do something?"

"Like what?" Bella replied.

"Well, do you think we can trust Sylvie?"

Bella looked to the cabin. "There's a reason that Kareema Ashburton picked her out to be her personal doctor, so I think we should respect her decision. Sylvie will know best how Kareema wants to be treated."

A twig snapped nearby.

Harriet swung around, convinced there was somebody there. But there was nothing but trees. They were the only people in the forest.

George spoke this time. "You think it was a mistake for us to take Kareema to hospital?"

Bella shrugged. "You weren't to know . . . but given Sylvie's rush to get Kareema away as soon as possible, then maybe. Yeah."

Harriet's chest tightened. "Do you think Kareema believes in alternative medicine — something like that?"

"Maybe," Bella replied.

They remained where they were for another ten minutes or so. It was then that Harriet heard a car engine approaching. A few minutes later, she observed Cassandra and Robert jogging along the path, making their way to the cabin. When they closed in, they looked exhausted. Their eyes sunken in their sockets. And their complexions were pale, despite the glorious sunlight.

Harriet couldn't help but think she must look even worse than they did.

From Cassandra and Robert's knowing silence, Harriet assumed Bella had filled them in over the phone. Harriet knew neither of them had any intention of saying anything which might break the well-balanced silence.

They might've waited outside the cabin for hours, or just for a few more minutes.

Time seemed to stretch out before Harriet — never-ending.

When Sylvie finally ushered them inside, Harriet had the urge to hold back.

She didn't want to go in.

She didn't feel *worthy* enough to go in.

Seeing her hanging back from the group, and seemingly reading her mind, Sylvie took hold of her by the elbow, and jostled her in behind the others. Harriet had to admit she felt like something of a fool to have to be taken by the arm, but thinking about it some more, she might never have made it inside without the forceful prompting.

Inside the cabin, the air smelled strongly of peppermint. There was something warm and wafting — infusing tea? — which rippled through the air. Harriet felt a ticklish sensation passing up the back of her neck, and her heart wallowed in her throat. She wanted nothing more than to step out of the Cottage — to be allowed to walk alone, back to the waiting car. She felt entirely unworthy to be here.

To stand before what might prove to be Kareema Ashburton's deathbed.

Sylvie seemed to sense the misgiving in the room. She brought the door shut, sealing them inside. The sun disappeared behind a cloud, and the darkness seemed somehow to accentuate Kareema's position where she lay on the camp bed.

When Kareema spoke, Harriet couldn't help but wonder if Sylvie hadn't given her some sort of drug to improve her strength. Her voice, although frail, carried through the room — easily understood by all.

"I have made my decision," Kareema said. "I want to do every-thing . . . everything in my power to help Humble progress. It . . . it is a worthy . . . *worthy* cause. One which has been borne in faith, and which will be carried forward in love . . . in the love you have for one . . . one another . . ."

Kareema drew a sharp breath in through her teeth. Her body seemed far weaker than Harriet had previously appreciated. It seemed as if a simple touch might be enough to break her bones. Although she had managed this far, it was clear that her strength was deserting her. She was slowly sinking back into the pillows of her camp bed — sinking away from the present . . . from life.

Bella spoke next. "I . . . really, I don't know what to say . . . we are —"

Kareema's frail voice rose again. "There is no reason to be grateful . . . I do this for my own reasons . . . for my own pleasure . . . and you were all . . . all . . . kind enough to give me another . . . another glimpse of my . . . my youth . . . when I rode that . . . that horse . . . I felt my childhood coming . . . . coming back to me . . . in a rush . . . too much to handle . . . I suppose."

It was then Harriet noticed the tears which ran down Kareema's cheeks. When Harriet brought her hand up to cover her own face, she realised she too was crying. She stole a look about the others, seeing they were similarly moved.

As Kareema lay before them, taking her last breaths, Harriet heard the final word which passed her lips.

"Thank you."

EPILOGUE

The storm clouds had let off all afternoon, but Harriet was unconvinced they wouldn't burst the moment she set foot outside the front door.

It would be just her *luck*.

Bella had told Harriet she could make her way into work whenever she wanted that day — they had all certainly put in a great deal of overtime in the past few weeks — and Harriet had used this licence as an excuse to keep herself out of the way of the brewing rainstorm. There was no time for her to waste any longer, though. They were planning to meet with Sylvie at three o'clock, and it was quarter to now.

Harriet was just going to have to chance it.

As she passed through the front hall, Maximilian winding himself about her calves, she pulled out the largest golf umbrella Aunt Adiema kept. Then she pulled on the raincoat and waterproof boots her aunt reserved for days such as these. It was strange to think that her aunt hadn't taken them with her today — but, then again, her aunt had never much bought into the idea of hoping for the best and preparing for the worst.

Sure enough, Harriet had no sooner brought the front door shut behind her than great big raindrops began to splatter the path. She scuttled along the pavement, doing a zig-zag as she went, as if it might be able to save her from the rain.

When she reached Molinaar's Cottage, she felt a strange sense of hesitation hit her. As if she shouldn't go any further. As if she would be intruding if she went inside the house. But she cleared away the doubt from her mind . . . this might be Bella, Robert and Cassandra's home, but it was also her place of work — and as the others had tried time and again to instil in her, she was just as welcome here as any of them were.

Somehow she had even managed to shake herself out of the habit she had acquired of knocking on the door. She simply turned the handle and went inside.

Everybody was sat around the kitchen table: Bella, Robert, Cassandra, and — of course — George. In the corner, Woss was snoozing away, his head resting on his crossed paws. The scene would've carried a relaxing charm to it if it hadn't been for the knowledge Harriet had of what they were expecting . . . that they were waiting for Sylvie.

That they were waiting for clarification.

On the future of Humble Greetings.

On their *own* futures.

Harriet had hardly had the chance to say a word when there was a knock on the door.

It was Bella who got up to go and answer. She scurried to the front hall, and Harriet heard her give Sylvie an overly enthusiastic greeting which betrayed her nervousness.

When Sylvie trod into the kitchen — on Bella's heels — Harriet saw she looked a little better rested, albeit with a couple of dark circles beneath each of her eyes. Her hair wasn't quite as immaculate as it usually was; with the odd strand hanging off here or there. She hovered over the offered chair before sitting herself down.

Harriet saw she carried a briefcase with her, and for a few seconds found it difficult to take her eyes off it.

Now sat down, Sylvie raised a half-smile. "Thank you for agreeing to meet with me."

"Thank you for meeting with *us*," Bella replied.

Sylvie's smile waned. "It's been a tough month — *hectic*, really. Even though there was so much time to prepare, you're never quite ready when the time comes, are you? Always some unexpected problem — something which needs sorting out urgently." She smiled again. "And Humble Greetings, I suppose, is that 'something urgent' today."

There was a nervous bout of laughter.

When Harriet laughed herself, she felt as if she might cry. She thought of the circumstances under which they had last seen Sylvie — how after Kareema Ashburton had . . . gone, Sylvie had told them that they should all leave too.

That she would make 'arrangements'.

They had known nothing else except for what had come out in the newspapers — nothing more than the broad strokes of Kareema's obituary.

"Now," Sylvie said, "as I'm sure you will have picked up on, Kareema named me her successor. I spent several years living in close quarters with Kareema — her personal doctor — and it was always her intention that I continue her work until such a time as I pass it on to the next in line." She glanced down at the briefcase at her feet. "Well, that being said, she did also inform me that I was quite entitled to do what I will with her . . . uh, *operations* . . . that she trusted me to do what I felt was the *right* thing."

Harriet glanced to George. He was staring directly at her. Harriet flushed slightly then looked away.

Sylvie bent down and retrieved the briefcase, setting it upon the table top. She undid the catches and then riffled through a pile of papers. "Now, I know Kareema had her ways — that she *believed* in the goodness of people — but she was quite insistent I should run what was once hers in my own image. That I should under no circumstances feel beholden to her legacy . . . to her way of doing things." She removed the papers from within the briefcase. "And, with that in mind, it is my opinion that any business arrangement should be accompanied by at least a *smattering* of paperwork. Just something for . . ."

"A rainy day," Robert put in, finishing her sentence.

Sylvie glanced to him, smiled. "Precisely." She flipped through the pages, and then passed them to Cassandra, sitting beside her.

Cassandra — in turn — gave them to Robert, with the urgency of a novice handling a very poisonous snake.

Robert smiled broadly and openly, weighing the pages in his hands.

"Everything is ready to go," Sylvie continued, doing up the briefcase and then getting up from her seat. "You will see that everything is in order — that the nature of the agreement you struck with Kareema is all there."

"Oh," Bella said, "won't you stay for some tea?"

Sylvie took a step backwards, towards the door. "I'm afraid not — I have some other engagements to see to. But it goes without saying that I wish you all the best in the world, and I hope that this arrangement helps you on the way to achieving your dreams. All of your dreams." She finally settled on George. "And you take it easy, all right? Do those exercises the physio set you, no matter how boring they seem."

And, with that, leaving everybody around the kitchen table stunned, Sylvie left.

The only sound in the kitchen now was the rustling of paper as Robert flipped his way through the pages Sylvie had handed him. He wore an expression of deep concentration as he skimmed the text, absorbing it all, analysing it all . . .

"How does it look?" Bella asked tentatively.

Robert finished off his current page then glanced up. "It looks good so far — but let me read it all the way through before I make any final judgement."

"Does it look good enough to celebrate?"

Robert thought about this for a long second, then said, "Yes, I should say so."

"Great! Then I'll go fetch the champagne."

Harriet looked across the table at George. He motioned in the direction of the garden. There was no need for him to ask her a second time. The two of them left the kitchen — with Robert leafing through the contract, Bella digging in the fridge for champagne, Cassandra sketching away on a scrap of paper, and Woss dreaming away, oblivious.

Outside, it had stopped raining. The thunderclouds had cleared and birdsong filled the air. The sun was breaking through.

Harriet breathed in the thick scent of berries and honey.

She could feel a warmth in the pit of her gut, and an enormous sense of inner strength rippled through her blood. It was like she could do anything she wanted now. She had only to raise herself to the challenge, and she would be able to do it.

She thought about how much she had learned in the course of the past few months with George at her side, and it was a dizzying realisation to think she would learn so much more. And that she would channel all her passions into him.

George took hold of her hand, and the two of them walked around the garden. Harriet had slipped off her shoes back in the kitchen and so she felt the bouncy, damp, tender grass on her bare soles. She couldn't recall a time when she had been happier.

Did life get any better than this?

When they got to a trellis archway, woven with roses, they locked eyes.

She could feel his warm breath against her neck.

"This is everything I ever hoped for," he said. "Only I didn't know it until now."

Harriet felt her whole body seize up. She reached out for him, holding him tight to her. She saw him wince . . . not having wholly gotten over his injuries yet it seemed.

"I feel the same," she replied.

And then they kissed.

THE END

AUTHOR'S NOTE

Thank you for taking the time to read one of my books. If you would like to hear about my latest releases you can sign up for my newsletter here: www.essiepowers.com

Thanks for reading!

Essie Powers

Humble Meetings
The Second Humble Greetings Novel